## By Laura McHugh

*The Weight of Blood*

*Arrowood*

*The Wolf Wants In*

*What's Done in Darkness*

# WHAT'S DONE
# IN DARKNESS

# WHAT'S DONE
# IN DARKNESS

A NOVEL

LAURA McHUGH

RANDOM HOUSE

NEW YORK

Copyright © 2021 by Laura McHugh

Published in the United States by Random House, an imprint and division of Penguin Random House LLC, New York.

RANDOM HOUSE and the HOUSE colophon are registered trademarks of Penguin Random House LLC.

Library of Congress Cataloging-in-Publication Data
Names: McHugh, Laura, author.
Title: What's done in darkness: a novel / Laura McHugh.
Description: First Edition. | New York: Random House, 2021.
Identifiers: LCCN 2020036215 (print) | LCCN 2020036216 (ebook) |
ISBN 9780399590313 (Hardcover) | ISBN 9780399590337 (Ebook)
Classification: LCC PS3613.C5334 W53 2021 (print) | LCC PS3613.C5334 (ebook) |
DDC 813/.6—dc23
LC record available at https://lccn.loc.gov/2020036215
LC ebook record available at https://lccn.loc.gov/2020036216

Printed in Canada on acid-free paper

randomhousebooks.com

2 4 6 8 9 7 5 3 1

First Edition

*For my sisters*

# WHAT'S DONE IN DARKNESS

# SARABETH, THAT DAY

## AGE 17

The blacktop road stretched empty in either direction, the sky hazy and the air heavy as a sodden sponge. The heat of the late-morning sun amplified the autumn scent of drying cornstalks, the putrid sweetness of persimmons rotting in the ditch. Insects swarmed the fermenting fruit, buzzing like an unholy plague. Sarabeth brushed away a sweat bee. She had walked the long, twisting path from the house to the roadside stand alone, pulling a wagon with one bad wheel, her legs sweating beneath her heavy ankle-length skirt.

Her little sister, Sylvie, sometimes worked the family's produce stand with her, but today she was home in bed with a fever and a vicious sore throat. Their mother had spent the early-morning hours praying over Sylvie and coaxing her to swallow a concoction of garlic, cider vinegar, and honey. Mama was piling more quilts on the bed when Sarabeth left, aiming to sweat out the sickness, shushing Sylvie when she cried that she was too hot. Mama said fever was nothing compared to the fires of Hell, and maybe God liked to remind us. She said it to Sylvie, but Sarabeth knew it was meant for her.

She was glad to get away from the house, away from her mother and preparations for Saturday's dreaded birthday dinner. Much as she hated to see Sylvie sick, she hoped her sister's illness might force them to cancel. She'd been counting the days until her eighteenth birthday because her father had promised that she could sign up for classes at the community college, where her older brother, Eli, was studying agriculture. She'd thought of it as her ticket out. Then, when the course catalog she'd been waiting for finally arrived over the summer, Mama chucked it into the trash. *You'll be too busy taking care of your husband,* she'd said.

*But I don't have a husband,* Sarabeth had replied, and her parents had exchanged measured looks. Her father cleared his throat, a decisive rumble that swept aside all objections before he even began to speak. The man they'd chosen for her would be coming over for dinner on her birthday. She'd felt like kicking and screaming but knew her father would dismiss her as hysterical. *You can't make me,* she'd whispered instead. *I won't do it.* Her mother's eyes had gone round with shock and then narrowed. Daddy had unbuckled his belt regretfully. He didn't enjoy whippings, though he felt they were necessary at times, like when one of the children was disrespectful or defiant. More often than not, that child was Sarabeth. Her flesh was still tender from the last time. The belt made a hissing sound as it slid out of the loops one by one.

She should have seen it coming. Mama had been grooming her for this very thing for years, but she'd assumed that once she became an adult, she could make her own decisions. She'd move out, start a new life. She'd expected them to pressure her to stay in the church, to continue living at home, but somehow she hadn't expected them to force her into an arranged marriage against her will.

Eli was sympathetic but wouldn't argue on her behalf. Her best friend, Retta, couldn't grasp why she was so upset. The girls had been friends most of their lives because their mothers were in a women's prayer group together, and after her father's accident, Sarabeth's family had left Church of Christ the Redeemer to join Retta's family at the more stringent Holy Rock. They used to play with dolls on Saturday afternoons in Retta's basement while the women's group met upstairs. Even back then, Retta had liked to pair up the dolls and give them weddings and babies, though she wasn't allowed any boy dolls. Sarabeth had cut the hair off one of the girl dolls and stapled its skirt together between its legs to play the part of the groom. Following the vows, Retta had laid the groom on top of the bride, fully clothed, in a shoebox bed.

Retta had gotten engaged weeks ago, and in the time since, she'd talked about almost nothing but marriage and her future husband. She'd always been bubbly, her sentences punctuated with giggles. Now she giggled while she said things like "I wonder how Philip likes his eggs—boiled, scrambled, sunny-side up?" She'd twist her waist-length braid into elaborate configurations on top of her head while musing how Philip might want her to wear her hair.

Sarabeth couldn't muster any interest in Philip's choice of eggs or hairstyles, even for Retta's sake. While all the sermons of faith and obedience and fruitfulness had effortlessly seeped into Retta, they had sheeted right off Sarabeth. Her mother put part of the blame on herself: They'd come late to Holy Rock, her oldest daughter already irreparably damaged by basic cable and public school; no amount of discipline or prayer or physical labor had managed to reshape her imperfect soul. Sarabeth had come to think of her time on the farm as a sentence that she had to serve, one with an end date. Now it seemed like she'd have to plan an escape.

She unloaded the wagon, set the cash box beneath the folding table, and arranged what was left of the produce to look as pleasing as possible. Most of the late-season tomatoes had been ruined by hornworms. She dusted off the pumpkins with the hem of her dress and sat down on the five-gallon bucket that served as her chair. She wished she had a little battery-powered radio, the kind their neighbor, Mr. Darling, kept in his barn, but of course her parents wouldn't have allowed it. She had to settle for the ambient sounds of the countryside: crows shrieking, cornstalks rustling, the far-off hum of a combine reaping the fields.

There was nothing to do but wait. After a while, she got up and walked to the edge of the road, then stepped to the chipped yellow line at its center, turning in a circle to survey the horizon. The fields gave way to forested ridges that faded to blue in the distance. She wondered what would happen if she picked a direction and started walking. How far would she get? Would someone offer her a ride? Would she take it?

The humming grew louder—not a combine this time, but a car, off to the west and moving closer. She tried to guess who might be inside. Maybe it was the elderly woman from town who would always buy a single tomato and slip Sylvie a piece of stale candy (or, once, a fuzzy cough drop) from the bottom of her purse. Maybe it was Jack, who'd been one of her best friends back when she lived in town and attended Wisteria Middle School. He and his buddies would stop sometimes, pile out of his Jeep, rifle through the produce. They made dirty gestures with the cucumbers and laughed at whispered jokes, watching for her reaction while Jack channeled silent apologies with his eyes. Jack had come alone once, not that long ago, but she knew that wouldn't happen again.

Sarabeth returned to her post behind the table and hiked up her skirt to feel the breeze on her legs, wishing for the millionth time that she could wear shorts like she used to, like normal people did when it was hot. The vehicle popped up on the crest of the far hill before dipping out of sight again, and then it reappeared close enough for her to see that it was a truck, gray or silver, or maybe beige or dirty white. Unfamiliar. A tiny thrill sparked in her chest. It was rare to see anyone new. Maybe they were city people, the type who would ask whether everything was organic and then take pictures of themselves standing in the corn to post on social media. She wasn't allowed to use social media—her parents didn't have internet access or even a computer—but Tom Darling used to let her look at his Instagram. Tom kept his account private, no followers, no selfies. His pictures were all of roosters and weathervanes and spiderwebs, familiar things that he managed to capture in unexpected ways. He had what Mr. Darling called "an artistic eye," though it didn't sound like a compliment the way he said it.

The truck rolled onto the gravel shoulder, no blinker, and she stood up to play the role she'd been taught. Be pleasant and helpful. Smile, but in a wholesome way that could not be perceived as flirtatious. The smile was automatic now, even when she felt like screaming.

The truck door opened, the engine still running, and a man got out. He wore a baseball cap with the bill pulled down, and with the sun behind him, it was hard to see his face, though it looked a bit strange. She didn't want to stare, to make him uncomfortable if he had some sort of affliction or deformity.

"Good morning," she said, her gaze partially lowered as he approached. His skin appeared rubbery, melted, as though he'd been burned in a fire. He was nearly within arm's reach when she realized he was wearing a mask.

It took a moment for the synapses to fire, for understanding to flicker through the neural pathways and set off alarms. She wondered if he meant to rob her, if she should offer him the thin stack of bills from the cash box. It wasn't until his gloved hand shot out that she wheeled and ran. There was nowhere to go but the field behind her or the long gravel road that led home. She darted into the corn, the dry leaves clawing her face, and felt herself wrenched backward as the man caught hold of her dress. She screamed.

A glove clamped over her mouth and nose, the leather reeking of sweat and sawdust. She bit, twisted, flung elbows, choked on her own tongue. The man pressed her to his chest, his breath seeping through her hair down to her scalp. His hand let go for an instant to grab something from his pocket and she cried out, the sound sharp and brief. There was a flicker of shadows, the crows taking flight overhead, and then nothing.

# CHAPTER I

# SARAH, NOW

S*arabeth*. Three syllables, hushed, like a secret whispered in my ear, my skin prickling as though I had felt his breath through the phone. The man was still talking, but it was all static after *Sarabeth*. No one called me that anymore. It was an old name. A dead name. I had been Sarah for nearly five years, and those who knew my real name never had cause to utter it, because they no longer spoke to me.

There was a pause while the man waited for me to respond. "Hello?" he said. "Are you there?"

I pressed my free hand flat against the cool metal desktop and tried to anchor myself in the present. My cluttered office at the animal shelter. The brightly colored sticky notes framing my monitor, reminding me of upcoming foster appointments. The mournful wail of a bloodhound in the exam room down the hall. I forced air into my constricted lungs, the stinging scent of bleach and urine filtering in as the kennels were sprayed down.

"I'm sorry," I said, my voice snagging in my throat. "I couldn't hear you."

"I'm Nick Farrow with the Missouri Highway Patrol, Missing Persons Unit. I need to speak with you about your case."

I swallowed hard, my mouth suddenly dry. Why would the Missouri state police be calling me now? I'd been found in Missouri, not far from the Arkansas line, but the Clayton County Sheriff's Department back in Wisteria had been in charge of the case, and after making a mess of it, they'd done their best to bury it and move on.

"Did something happen?" I asked. "Has something new come up?"

"Not exactly," he said. "Not in regard to your case specifically. But there's a missing person case that bears some resemblance to yours. I'd like to ask you a few questions."

"I'm sorry," I said. "It was a long time ago. I've already given all the information I had."

I sensed skepticism in his silence and wasn't surprised. I knew it was difficult to believe that I'd been held captive for more than a week yet didn't know who'd taken me or where I'd been. People had their own ideas about what had happened to Sarabeth Shepherd, the seventeen-year-old girl who'd vanished from her family's farm in rural Arkansas and reappeared in a bloodstained slip along Highway 65, bound and blindfolded, with a dubious story about how she ended up there. I thought of that Sarabeth as a different person altogether, the girl from the newspaper headlines.

"I understand," Farrow said in a gentle Good Cop voice, his tone implying *I am on your side.* I knew from experience that if you didn't give Good Cop what he wanted, it was only a matter of time before Bad Cop stepped in. *Did you run away, Sarabeth? Did you cause these injuries yourself? Cut off your own hair? Did you make it all up for attention?*

"I still want to talk to you," Farrow continued. "I know it's been a while, but some things have changed since then."

The bloodhound's cries grew louder as Melissa, my boss, led him past my office toward the outdoor runs. The dog twisted and squirmed, fighting the leash. We'd found him tied to the fence when we arrived to open the shelter an hour ago, his ears lumpy with ticks. It was all too common for people to dump animals overnight, to avoid the intake fee or the paperwork or the discomfort of looking someone in the eye while they relinquished a pet. Last August, we'd found a litter of twelve black kittens sealed in a plastic storage tub in the parking lot. All but one had perished in the heat before we got to them. Melissa named the survivor Sunny and bottle-fed her around the clock for days, but she didn't make it.

"What's changed?" I asked.

"We've got new tools, technologically speaking," he said. "I'm sure you've seen it in the news. Software that can link crimes. Genealogical databases that can help identify criminals from cold cases. There's a chance we could find the person who took you."

He dangled that vague possibility as though it would entice me. I had left my old life behind on the farm, like the snakes that shed their skins in the fields, a process necessary for survival. A piece of me was still there in Arkansas, but I was gone. No one in my new life knew who I was, what had happened to me, and I wanted to keep it that way.

"You said this was about another case."

"Yes," he said. "A sixteen-year-old girl went missing from a small town near the Bootheel. No trace of her since, no sightings, nothing. I'm checking for any possible connection to previous abductions, and I need your help. An hour of your time."

"Do you think she might have run away?"

There was a sound like paper shuffling. A muted sigh. I wondered if he remembered the news coverage of my case, if he'd been working in missing persons back then. Regardless, he'd have read enough of the file to be aware of the lingering suspicion that I was responsible for my own disappearance. I wasn't the only survivor in recent years to be accused of pulling a real-life *Gone Girl*, to fail the purity test for girls who come back alive. Sheriff Krieger had chuckled when I said I couldn't describe the suspect or the location because I'd been blindfolded the entire time and kept in the dark. *Is that right*, he said, his shoulders ratcheting up and down as he laughed. *Well, ain't that convenient.*

"We can't rule it out," Farrow said. "But no, I don't think she ran away."

I stared at a neon-green Post-it: *Helen, Dairy Queen, Worm X.* My most prolific volunteer would be arriving soon to get her latest foster puppies dewormed. The Dairy Queen litter. They'd been found in a dumpster behind the restaurant.

"What makes you think I can help?"

"She has some things in common with you, Sarabeth."

"Sarah," I said. "I go by Sarah now." He knew that, no doubt, and used my old name purposefully, in an attempt to dredge up the past, to haul painful memories to the surface, foul and dripping. I thought of my brothers playing at the muddy edge of the farm pond one spring, poking hibernating frogs to wake them. *Leave them be!* my little sister, Sylvie, had piped. *They're dreaming.* Sylvie wouldn't be little like I remembered her. She'd be sixteen now, my brothers grown into men.

"Sarah," he said, his voice softening. "You might have a valuable piece of information without realizing it. Something that could help us find her. *You* could bring her home."

He stated it with conviction, as though it was a real possibility, but he was wrong. I couldn't save anyone. Five years later, my own survival still seemed tenuous. I'd stopped taking pills for anxiety and insomnia, not because I didn't need them anymore, but because I worried they made me less alert. I had nightmares, the fear so visceral that I felt no relief even when I woke in my own bed, the night-light burning brightly enough to illuminate the familiar landscape of my bedroom.

"I wish I could help, I really do."

"You can. All I'm asking—"

"Look, I'm at work," I said. "It's not a good time."

"Wait," he said. "Her name's Abby Donnelly."

"I'm sorry, I have to go."

"Think about it," he said. "Think about Abby. I'll be in touch."

I hung up, chilled by the sweat that had dampened my skin during the brief conversation. I didn't know for sure whether Farrow could compel me to talk to him, but I told myself that he couldn't. I pressed my palms to the desk, breathed in the scent of disinfectant, clamped my tongue between my teeth. *You're okay. You're safe.* Despite the rituals of reassurance, I felt wobbly, like my bones had gone soft. I kept Sarabeth buried as best I could, but the grave was shallow and easily disturbed.

"Hey," Melissa said, pushing the door open with her elbow, an armful of crusty-eyed kittens clutched against her substantial bosom. "I need somebody to drive a crate of baby raccoons to the wildlife rehab. If we're not there by five they lose their spot." She made kissy faces at the kittens, murmuring baby talk. "And coccidia is spreading through the holding room again. Think Helen'll take another sick litter?"

I tried to wrench my attention back to where it needed to be.

Orphaned raccoons. Sick kittens. Problems I could actually do something about.

Melissa glanced over at me and frowned, her foundation creasing across the bridge of her nose. She was still wearing her summer shade, a tawny beige applied liberally from hairline to jawbone, though her neck and arms revealed the paleness of early October. Her bleached hair was gelled back into a banana clip, exposing the paw-print tattoo behind her ear, and a purple fitness tracker cut into the flesh of her wrist. The Fitbit had been a gift from her ex, a trainer who was always nagging her about diet and exercise, and from what I could tell, Melissa continued to wear it out of spite. *Oh, look at that, asshole!* she'd mutter. *Ten thousand freaking steps before noon.*

"You sick?" she asked. "You look awful."

Melissa could be counted on to speak truthfully, if not tactfully.

"Really? I feel fine."

She arched an eyebrow and took a step back. "If you're sick, don't spread it around." Melissa had endless sympathy and tolerance for sick animals but couldn't stand to be ill herself. She was still bitter about the time she caught swine flu and missed both the holiday adoption rush and the end-of-year office party.

"I'm good," I said, almost convincingly. "Just one of those days."

"One of those days?" She studied my face, probably trying to determine whether I was developing a contagious fever or simply having a rough morning. Her expression softened. "Why don't you go check on the cat room," she said. "The volunteer didn't show up."

An excuse to play with the animals—Melissa's version of therapy. She had no formal medical training, but she had good instincts and could sense when something wasn't quite right, like when a kitten was about to fade or an employee was on the verge of a breakdown. She was a good boss, and I was grateful that she'd taken a chance on me.

I'd shown up for my interview the same day an animal hoarder's house had caught fire, and intake was swamped with cats and dogs in various states of neglect. Melissa had pulled me into the back immediately and was impressed by my stoicism during the onslaught of filth, wounds, and bared teeth. I had grown up on a farm, had seen worse things.

I was nervous, at first, that someone at the shelter might recognize me from the news, though by then more than two years had passed since I'd been in the headlines, and I didn't particularly resemble the old photo that had been circulated when I was found: teenage me at a church revival in an old-fashioned prairie dress, barefaced, sandy hair that hung all the way to my hips. By the time I started my job, my hair had grown out a bit from the drastic cut that had been necessary after the uneven shearing I'd endured in captivity, but I never let it get past my shoulders. I had dropped the extra syllable from my first name and gotten rid of Shepherd altogether, replacing it with my middle name.

I needn't have worried. There were no sideways glances, no whispers, no one telling me that I looked familiar. A few months ago, a new vet tech named Karim had tilted his head when I popped in for an update on a spaniel, his index finger tapping his lips. He had the charismatic smile of a talk-show host, and when he focused his attention on me, it gave me the uneasy sensation of standing onstage in a blinding spotlight. He turned his finger toward me, pointing. "Are you from the Bootheel?" I'd frozen in place, and he mistook my fear for confusion. "Your accent," he said, grinning.

I shook my head, looking down at his sneakers to avoid his smile. "Arkansas."

"Oh, Little Rock?" I'd learned that Little Rock was the only place in Arkansas anyone not from Arkansas had heard of.

"No," I said. "A small town. You wouldn't know it."

Karim started to reply, but I'd mumbled an excuse and darted out. The next few times I saw him, he'd tried to engage in friendly conversation, but I always cut it short. I was too worried that he'd bring up Arkansas again, that he would somehow connect invisible dots and guess my secret. He still smiled at me, warmth and charm radiating from him like cartoon sunbeams, but he spoke carefully now, in soft tones and only about work, his movements slow and deliberate, as though trying not to spook a skittish animal.

I hurried past the exam room to avoid running into Karim or any of the other techs and let myself into the cat room. Kitten season was still going strong thanks to the warm weather, and most of the cages were full of adorable fluff balls that would have no trouble getting adopted. The older cats were a tougher sell. I knelt to check on a scrawny orange tabby named Mr. Marmalade, who was yowling and digging at his cage door. He was a stray from the Swan Lake trailer park, used to roaming free. He tried to squeeze through the narrow gap as I eased the door open, but I managed to catch him and hoist him up, each knob of his spine protruding beneath his fur.

"I get it," I murmured. "It's no fun being locked up." He tensed and drove his claws into my chest, ready to launch himself out of my arms, and I hastily maneuvered him back into his cage. "I'm sorry," I said, clicking the latch. "I hope you get out of here soon."

I spotted a plump tortoiseshell kitten that reminded me of a mama cat we'd had on the farm. Sylvie had liked to give her milk in the fancy china saucer we'd rescued when Mama threw out the last of our grandmother's things. We watched the cat birth a litter of kittens in our barn, the newborns squeaking and trembling, eyes sealed shut, blind to the world.

I hadn't wondered back then, but I did now—what it was like when their eyes opened for the first time. If the light was painful or frightening or if it felt like a miracle, like when I emerged from days of darkness, my blindfold torn away to reveal a pink sky over a trash-strewn highway rest stop. The light had been soft and unbearably beautiful, and it made me squint. I'd hoped that it was sunrise and not sunset, because I couldn't bear the thought of the dark returning so soon. As I lay on the cold gravel, the sun grew brighter and brighter and I'd thought of Pastor Rick's sermons on the Resurrection and figured this was as close as I'd ever get to being born again and starting a new life. I had thought, in those first moments of daylight, that I'd put the darkness behind me.

Helen swept in at eleven with a crate of freshly bathed puppies, the air in my office filling with the luxurious scent of her vetiver perfume. Helen's dark corkscrew curls haloed her face, a few threads of silver creeping in at the temples. Large princess-cut diamonds gleamed on her earlobes. I'd begged my mother to let me get my ears pierced when I turned thirteen, but she'd insisted that it was a sin to defile the body the Lord had given me.

*I used to save the good jewelry for special occasions, just like my mother did,* Helen had told me once when she caught me admiring the earrings. *But now I figure waking up in the morning is reason enough.* She'd squeezed my arm and laughed warmly.

Helen might have looked more glamorous than the typical shelter volunteer, but her appearance didn't get in the way of her work. She was the one we turned to for the most challenging cases. Helen would take the paralyzed terrier whose bladder and bowels had to be manually expressed; the Lab with such severe separation anxiety that he would tear apart any closed door. Helen could handle the ringworm cases, the amputees, the cats that needed Baytril injections or ointment that had to be applied directly to the eye.

"Aren't they just darling?" she said, reaching into the crate to extract a sleek black pup not much bigger than her hand.

"Yes," I said, stroking the smooth fur, noting the cushion of fat beneath. "Much better shape than when they came in. So what theme did you decide on?"

"Greek mythology," Helen said, rising to add their names to the list on the whiteboard. *Dairy Queen litter: Ares, Artemis, Athena, Persephone, Zeus, Apollo.*

"I considered dairy-inspired names, given their provenance, but I didn't get very far down that road." She snapped the cap back on the marker. "Nothing wrong with being aspirational."

I eyed the running totals on the board. "You're beating Dave and Evelyn," I said. "You're a lock for most fosters again this year."

Helen smiled, perfect veneers gleaming. "Oh, it's not a competition, is it?"

"Evelyn thinks it is."

She laughed. "Just give her the plaque. I don't have room on my wall for another one."

That wasn't true. I had seen bits of Helen's home in the photos she posted on the foster page, and from what I could tell, she was not lacking in space. She bathed dogs in an enormous farmhouse sink in an airy kitchen with endless, uncluttered marble

countertops. Cats lounged in a vaulted sunroom filled with potted citrus trees and an elaborate network of kitty condos. The
buff leather interior of her Mercedes appeared spotless in pictures despite numerous posts about animals having accidents in
the car when she took them home. *Poor Oscar had a rough
ride—how can such a tiny angel throw up so much?—but now
he's clean and dry and napping by the fire!* I envied the animals
sometimes—what it must be like to have Helen caring for them,
their surroundings safe and serene, any messes promptly tidied
up and forgiven.

"So what's new with *you?*" Helen asked as I got out the Worm
X, her brown eyes wide. She always asked how I was doing, if I
had fun plans for the weekend, always listened attentively to my
underwhelming responses, which were usually "fine" and "no."
On the rare occasions that I revealed something mildly personal,
like a visit to the botanical gardens for the orchid show, she
would say "*Oh,* tell me more." Helen was the closest thing I had
to a friend, though I would have been embarrassed for her to
know that.

The closeness was illusory. She texted me every day, but it
was mostly to share pictures and updates on her fosters. I knew a
lot about her, but nothing terribly personal. If I wrote it all down,
it would read like a breezy celebrity profile. She liked Louis Vuit-
ton bags, the bigger the better, and had a weakness for peanut
butter M&Ms. She was divorced, retired from some sort of ex-
ecutive position, and was now involved in philanthropy, serving
on various boards and attending countless charity galas.

"What's new with me?" I did my best to smother Nick Farrow's voice in my head, to ignore the memories flaring up like an
outbreak of hives. I squirted Worm X into the puppies' mouths,
one after another. "Nothing, really."

Helen tilted her head, concern welling in her eyes. "Are you all right?"

I stared at her, my skin itching, and wondered if my thoughts really had manifested in a rash, too virulent for my body to suppress them.

She touched her clavicle, pointed to mine with a long, lacquered fingernail. I'd never seen her without an impeccable manicure, each nail filed into the shape of a tiny coffin. "You're bleeding," Helen said.

I dabbed at the threads of dried blood where Mr. Marmalade had clawed me. The punctures were tender to the touch. "Oh — it's nothing. I'm fine." I forced a smile for her. "Just a stray who wanted out of his cage."

Helen immediately produced a wet wipe and a tube of antibiotic ointment from her massive purse. "The poor thing," she murmured, shaking her head. "It's traumatic, being locked up, don't you imagine? The stress and the fear. Changes a creature, makes them do things they wouldn't do in ordinary circumstances."

I couldn't argue.


The sun blazed in the rearview mirror as I drove home on a back road along pastures and cornfields. It felt deceptively like the countryside, even if the silhouettes of outlet malls and stadiums loomed in the distance. St. Agnes, with its quaint brick streets and farmers markets, was less than twenty minutes from downtown St. Louis. My neighborhood was nestled on the west bank of the Missouri River, rows of small but cozy Depression-era bungalows with covered porches and shade trees.

My house was nearly identical to those tucked on either side of it, except for the thicket of lilac bushes that kept it hidden from the street. I liked the feeling of being surrounded by people while remaining invisible. I'd bought the place with a settlement from the Clayton County Sheriff's Department, which had treated me like a criminal from the beginning, spreading baseless claims to the media that I'd faked my own abduction. Meanwhile, they lost the one piece of evidence that might have proven them wrong. I hadn't wanted the lawsuit, fearing it would only draw more attention, but the counselor and the lawyer from the Midwest Victims Advocacy Network had explained that it was in my best interest, given my limited options and resources. They'd gotten me out of Arkansas and into a temporary shelter, but I had no diploma, no job experience aside from working on the farm, no one to provide references or co-sign for a loan.

I'd spent most of my first two years in St. Agnes holed up in the house taking online courses, earning my GED (as it turned out, my homeschool certificate had not been legitimate) and an associate's degree, and learning how to do normal adult things like drive a car and manage a bank account. After I graduated, Casey, my counselor, had gently suggested that it might be time to integrate myself into society—meet people, make friends, get a job—not just because the settlement money wouldn't last forever, but because if I continued to confine myself inside my own four walls, wasn't I in a sense still trapped? For years on my family's farm, and then later in that dark room, I had longed to be out in the world, living free, but when given the chance, I'd voluntarily imprisoned myself. *There's no one holding you back now,* Casey had said, *except you.*

My foster dog, Gypsy, a 120-pound mastiff, whined and clawed at her crate when I walked in. I let her out into the backyard and she ran the perimeter, sniffing along the privacy fence, trampling what remained of the late-blooming zinnias in the flower beds. She had arrived at the shelter with jagged pink scars across her face, a milky eye, and a wariness of men, but given time to warm up, she'd proven loyal and sweet. In the three months I'd had her, no one had shown any interest in adopting her. Her appearance was intimidating, the lingering evidence of her secret trauma scaring people away. Her scars didn't bother me. I didn't mind when people saw us coming and cut a wide berth. I felt safer with her around.

The sun fell below the fence and the warmth vanished with it. It would be harvest time back on the farm, the fields glowing gold in the slanted light. I whistled for Gypsy to come inside, and she lay with her head on my feet while I ate dinner and watched TV. When it was time for bed, she curled up in her crate and I began my nightly ritual, walking through the house room by room, peering into closets and behind curtains, turning off lights, checking each door and window to make sure it was securely locked. The white walls were splotched here and there with various shades of green paint from seafoam to teal, as though the previous owners couldn't decide which color they liked best and gave up. The realtor had breezily remarked that it would be easy to paint over, but I hadn't bothered. In the years that I'd lived here, the only things I'd hung on the wall were a Humane Society calendar from work and a chalkboard that I'd thought I would write things on but never did. It remained a pristine black void, like a window looking out on a perpetually starless night.

There were no framed pictures, no family photographs. For the last several years that I lived at home, my family hadn't owned a camera. My mother insisted that photographs were vain and unnecessary. To my knowledge, not a single picture of my whole family—my three brothers, my sister, Sylvie, our parents, and me—existed. I had a photo of Sylvie holding a chicken at the Darlings' farm when we were helping to gather eggs. Tom Darling had taken it with his grandmother's Polaroid, and I kept the picture in a small album in my nightstand, not daring to expose it to light, lest it fade.

I climbed into bed with my laptop and, in the safety of my room, allowed myself to think about Farrow and the things he had said. I avoided the news as much as possible, because it tended to make me feel anxious and overwhelmed, so I hadn't heard anything about the missing girl he had mentioned. I googled "Abby Donnelly Missouri," trying different spellings of the first and last names, and when nothing relevant came up, I typed "Abby missing." The top hits were for Abby Hernandez, who had been held captive for nine months before being released and leading police to her captor. The further I scrolled, the more missing Abbys came up. Too many. But no Abby Donnelly.

I put the laptop away and took the photo album from my nightstand drawer. The picture of Sylvie was on the first page. My sister's long hair streamed loosely over her shoulder, dark gold like molasses, hazel eyes squinting in the light, sunburn pinking her cheeks and nose. Her mouth wide with laughter. I tried to remember the sound of her laugh and couldn't be sure that I had it right.

I flipped through the rest of the pages, all of them blank, until I found the envelope I'd stashed near the back, postmarked Wisteria, Arkansas, the address penned in my mother's handwriting. I unfolded the single sheet of notebook paper inside.

Dear Sarabeth,

Your sister Sylvia is engaged to be married, and it is

her wish to invite you to the wedding, to have her family join together in celebrating this blessed occasion.

I'd read the letter over and over in the days since I'd received it, and each time my heart withered at the thought of Sylvie getting married at sixteen. I'd thought I would bring her to live with me someday, that I could rescue her, like I had been rescued. Give her a chance to live her own life. Now I was too late.

I'd wished so many times that I could call her, talk to her, but our parents had gotten rid of the phone after I left. Too many reporters calling. I wrote to them, but news from home was rare and filtered through Mama, like the letter about the engagement. *We are overjoyed by the path God has chosen for your sister.* Of course Mama was overjoyed, but what about Sylvie?

I blamed myself. Maybe if I had stayed and gotten married, they wouldn't be forcing this on her so soon. No way I could sit in the audience at my sister's wedding without screaming objections and trying to drag her out of the church. I hadn't written back yet, hadn't decided what I was going to do.

I returned the letter to its hiding place, put the album back in the drawer, and switched off the lamp. *No nightmares,* I whispered to myself. *No nightmares, no nightmares, no nightmares.* I kept a night-light burning, just bright enough to reveal the outlines of my dresser, chair, and bookcase, so that I'd immediately know where I was if I woke up in the night. I wasn't afraid of the dark after what had happened. It wasn't the dark itself that threatened but the things hidden beneath its shroud, and some of those things moved just as easily in daylight.

# CHAPTER 2

# SARABETH, THEN

## AGE 14

"I made this for you." Mama stepped into the bedroom I shared with Sylvie and handed me a booklet covered with flowered shelf paper. I opened it, noting the care she'd taken with the booklet's construction, how she'd folded the sticky paper into sharp points at each corner and pasted a piece of sturdy white paper inside the front cover. My name was printed there in ballpoint pen. *Sarabeth Shepherd.*

The first page was filled with Mama's slanted handwriting. When I was younger, I'd watch her write out our weekly chore chart and imagine that her slanted words were in a hurry, hunched forward and walking purposefully, perhaps into a strong wind. In the booklet, each line was perfectly spaced, as though she'd placed a ruler beneath her pen as she wrote.

### GUIDE FOR GODLY GIRLS

1. Daddy is the head of our household, and we will be obedient and mindful of his headship at all times.

2. We will dress modestly and appropriately. Clothing must provide proper coverage and not cling to the flesh.
3. We will wear our hair long and abstain from cutting it. 1 Corinthians 11:15: "But if a woman have long hair, it is a glory to her: for her hair is given her for a covering."
4. We will learn and practice the womanly arts of the home, including cooking, sewing, cleaning, and childcare.
5. We will avoid unwholesome and unhealthy influences and activities in all forms.

I flipped through, wondering if the entire book was filled with rules, more than I'd be able to remember, let alone obey, but most of the pages were blank.

"You can use it to take notes in Bible study, write down prayers," she said. "You know, like a journal. I made one for Sylvie, too."

"Thank you," I said. I knew she had put a lot of effort into trying to make it pretty, though I wasn't sure why. Daddy was always preaching about the beauty of keeping things plain and simple, probably because we couldn't afford anything fancy or store-bought since he'd quit his job as a traveling salesman. I'd been using a spiral-bound notebook for Sunday school, my Bible study notes consisting mainly of doodles, expanding geometric patterns like Eli and I used to make with the Spirograph before Mama donated it, along with most of the other toys, to the Salvation Army. I wouldn't dare put my prayers down on paper, because I didn't doubt that my mother would open up the little book and read them. *Dear God, please let us move back to town.*

"I know you miss your friends from school," she said, squeezing my arm. "There have been lots of changes. But you'll understand one day, this is all for the best." Her skin was flushed with the excitement of her conviction, belief humming through her like an electric current. I felt the energy through the sleeve of my dress where her fingers gripped my flesh.

"Yes, ma'am," I said.

She nodded and released me, satisfied with my response. When she left, I placed the booklet next to my Bible on the otherwise-empty shelf. Mama had cleared out my Little House books after deciding that Laura Ingalls, despite her long hair and dresses, was impertinent, and then came back to confiscate the Chronicles of Narnia, which she had recently realized were fantasy books, despite my insistence that C. S. Lewis was a Christian author.

Three months after moving to the farm, the slant-ceilinged room still felt barren, uninviting. Two twin beds for me and Sylvie, each neatly made with plain white sheets and yellow polyester blankets. A shared dresser that had come with the house, the musty drawers holding our socks and underwear and the long dresses Mama had sewn for us, plus one that I'd sewn myself, the pleats of the skirt gathered incorrectly, the hem wildly uneven. The plank floor was covered with a homemade rag rug. In our old house, in town, my bedroom had baby-blue shag carpeting and puffy valances that looked like clouds, and my bookshelf had been packed tight with library books and board games.

We had been a fairly normal family. Mama was the religious one, a preacher's daughter. She stayed home with us while Daddy worked. We went to church and Sunday school and Bible study and Bible camp, but so did most everyone else we knew. I was in seventh grade at Wisteria Middle School when Daddy got into a terrible accident on the way home from his route, his sedan pleated up like an accordion between two semis, trapping him but miraculously leaving just enough room for him to survive. He blacked out and woke to flames, which he thought were the fires of Hell, and by the time the firemen cut him out of the car and whisked him into an ambulance, he'd had an epiphany.

He was a sinner, he said—he had actually lined us up on the couch, even the younger kids, and confessed, to our great discomfort and confusion, to lustful thoughts about a truck-stop waitress in Fayetteville—but God had saved him for some reason. It became clear to him, upon deep prayer and reflection, that he had been given a second chance at life for the sake of his family. He would rededicate himself to the Lord and do everything he could to protect us from the evils of the world and ensure that our souls were saved, so the next time flames rose up and he was plucked from this earthly life, it would be by God's hand, and not the Devil's pitchfork.

It seemed a bit extreme, and it made me wonder if Daddy had done more than fantasize about the waitress, if it was Mama rather than God who had forced his epiphany.

He sold our house in town and bought a small farm, where we could live simply and raise modest crops to survive. We joined Holy Rock, the church Retta's family belonged to, and Mama started homeschooling us. She replaced all my pants and Sylvie's with long skirts and dresses. The boys got to keep their sneakers, but when they wore out, they'd be replaced with ugly brown work boots.

In the beginning, it almost felt like an adventure, playing at being pioneers, like the Ingalls family in my Little House books. The novelty wore off quickly, like cheap varnish. I missed my school friends, the roller rink, sleepovers. I even missed things that had annoyed me before, like grocery shopping. I remembered sitting in the car one day after school while Mama ran into the Price Chopper for milk and cereal, hunched down in the seat so no one would see me at the cheaper of Wisteria's two grocery stores. I'd flipped between radio stations, wishing she'd hurry up, thinking that I couldn't possibly be more bored. Now I would have given anything to go to the store and run into someone I knew, to buy a box of Froot Loops and listen to the radio, to be surrounded by familiar comforts and feel like I was part of the outside world. At times the hunger for my old life flared into a desperate animal need to escape, and one night I had snuck out to see if I could walk to town, but it was so dark and we were so far from anything that I finally gave up and turned around.

"Hey." Eli leaned into the room, holding on to the doorframe. Mama had buzzed his hair too short the night before and it looked funny, his exposed scalp paler than his face, but that sort of thing didn't bother him. "Daddy said to go over to the Darlings and help with the walnuts."

We'd bought our land from Mr. and Mrs. Darling, whose son had owned it before he died. Their much larger farm bordered ours, and they were teaching us all the things we didn't know about homesteading, which was pretty much everything. They had loaned us equipment, helped with repairs, brought us food under the guise of Mrs. Darling getting overly ambitious with her canning. Daddy didn't like to accept charity or feel indebted to anyone, so he'd made a standing offer to help out whenever they needed an extra set of hands.

Mr. and Mrs. Darling would invite us over for a few simple chores and then find excuses for Eli and me to hang around. I had the feeling they did it for Tom, their grandson. He was two years younger than Eli and a year older than me, and he'd moved in with his grandparents after his father's arms were severed in a hay baler. Tom told us that his dad had survived the accident but later drowned himself in the pond because he didn't want to live without arms, unable to drive a tractor or manage livestock or do any of the things a farmer needs to do. Mr. Darling had said his son died from complications after the accident, not that he'd killed himself. I didn't know which version of the story was true.

Eli and I walked up the Darlings' gravel drive. Their farmhouse was nicer and prettier than ours, with a wide front porch and bay windows, the barn red with white trim and a weathervane on top, like something out of a picture book. Zinnias and sweet peas filled the flower beds on either side of the steps. Mrs. Darling liked to pick them and put bouquets in old pickle jars and perfume bottles all around the house, even in the bathroom. *The more you cut them*, she had told me, *the more they bloom.*

Tom was sitting on the steps waiting when we walked up. He swiped his wheat-colored hair away from his forehead and stood up to greet us, his gangly frame unfolding like the jointed paper skeleton we used to hang on our front door back when we still celebrated Halloween.

"Hey," he said, grinning, his head swiveling back and forth from me to Eli. "Grampa said we can take the Gator."

Tom had told us he knew how to operate every bit of machinery on the farm, including the combine and loader, but since the baler accident, the Gator was the only thing Mr. Darling would let him use. It resembled a golf cart, and while riding around the farm with Tom wasn't exactly like cruising the Wisteria strip with friends, it was as close as Eli and I would get.

We parked in a grove of walnut trees that bordered the pond. Knee-high weeds and sticker bushes grew unchecked all the way to the water's edge. "Watch out," Tom said. "It's hard to see the nuts in the grass. They'll roll your ankle if you step on 'em wrong."

I found one with my foot and picked it up, the rotted husk falling away from the shell, its odor pungent but not unpleasant.

"You guys didn't bring gloves?" Tom asked.

We shook our heads.

"Here," he said, handing me the pair he'd brought for himself. "Walnuts'll stain your hands worse than shoe polish."

"What about you?" I asked.

He shrugged. "Won't bother me none. Usually we get 'em in the fall, when the husks are still green. Grampa cracks 'em and Gramma puts 'em in her Christmas fudge. But we didn't get around to it last year."

I wondered if that was because of the pond, if Mr. and Mrs. Darling couldn't bear to go near the place where their son had drowned, assuming Tom's version of the story was true. It would be hard to have that reminder of death so close to home.

Tom kept his back to the pond as we worked, collecting the walnuts in a five-gallon bucket. He talked nonstop, like he'd been saving up things to say for a long time and didn't have anyone else to tell them to—and maybe he didn't. We'd figured out that we knew some of the same kids from town, but if he had friends other than Eli and me, he never mentioned them.

Tom stopped talking long enough to rub sweat off his face, leaving a dark smear across his forehead like a bruise, his nails stained black. "You guys wanna get some sodas?"

Eli hesitated, but I was already stripping off my gloves. "Sure," I said. "Thank you." Sodas were another relic of our past, though I wasn't certain if they'd been banished out of a general sense of austerity or if sugar and caffeine had crowded onto the list of sins.

We took the Gator back to the house and went in through the kitchen door. The boys scrubbed their hands and then Tom got Cokes out of the fridge. There were bouquets of flowers on the table, the windowsill, and the sideboard, where a green spider had strung a dainty web between a sweet pea blossom and the handle of a teacup.

"Gramma," Tom called into the sitting room. "The Shepherd kids are here."

There was creaking and shuffling as Mrs. Darling got up from her armchair and hobbled in. She wore a housedress with an embroidered apron over the top. "Sorry it took me a minute to say a proper hello," she said, rubbing her swollen knuckles. "Must've nodded off watching my stories." She glanced at the sweating red can in Eli's hand, and I instinctively moved to hide mine in the folds of my skirt, worried that she would snatch it away, that our mother had told her we weren't allowed.

"Tommy, are there any cookies left to put out for our guests?"

"No, ma'am," he said, his ears reddening.

She shook her head apologetically. "My arthritis has been acting up," she said. "Haven't been able to keep up with the baking. I swear we go through a loaf of bread and a dozen cookies a day."

Eli nudged his elbow into my arm. "Sarabeth is a great baker," he said. "If you're needing some help." I jabbed back at him. Since we no longer had the luxury of going to the store for a loaf of Wonder Bread, our mother had enlisted me to help with the baking, a dull and endless chore that meant hours in a sweltering kitchen under her constant scrutiny.

"Is that so?" Mrs. Darling asked.

Eli pressed his cold Coke against my back. I turned my head just enough to glare at him inconspicuously. He widened his eyes, dug the Coke into my kidney. Smiled. Put the can to his lips and took a long, blissful sip.

I got the message. There were more Cokes in the fridge, a whole row. I had seen them. Chocolate milk, too. And little cups of Swiss Miss butterscotch pudding like the ones Mama used to pack in our lunches in grade school. From the living room came the familiar strains of *The Young and the Restless* theme. Our grandma had watched it religiously. You could almost imagine, in the Darlings' kitchen, that life went on as before, that we were normal kids who could do normal things. I turned back to Mrs. Darling.

"I do love to bake," I said in my sweetest, most virtuous voice. "I'd be happy to help out, if you'd like."

Our father would not say no. He had deemed the Darlings Good Christian People, even if they did have a television, and he'd do almost anything to repay their compassion and generosity. I'd bake for them every day if it meant spending time in their kitchen instead of ours, drinking soda and listening to the TV, surrounded by reminders of the outside world, and, best of all, no one standing over me, lecturing me on all my failures, practical, spiritual, and otherwise.

Mrs. Darling's soft face spread into a smile, and her liver-spotted hand reached out to touch my cheek. "Oh, my child, you are an angel."

Tom beamed at Eli and me, his mouth stretched wide, showing all his teeth.

# CHAPTER 3

# SARAH, NOW

Gypsy and I had the riverfront trail to ourselves in the early-morning hours before work. I walked with the leash on my wrist, phone in one hand, Mace in the other. Fog hung low over the river as the sun rose through the trees to reveal a network of dew-spangled spiderwebs connecting the branches. The dampness seeped into my clothing and turned my skin clammy. Near the bridge, Gypsy pulled me to the edge of the trail, where the earth had begun to give way in muddy sloughs, sniffing at something I couldn't see. Down below, the brown water swirled and eddied along the bank, sucking debris into foaming whirlpools.

We were nearly home when I spied a black SUV parked in front of my house. The neighbor's teenage daughter had an endless stream of friends picking her up at the curb now that they were old enough to drive, but most of them drove beater cars plastered with bumper stickers, music blaring.

As we got closer, I noted details, just in case. Chevy Tahoe, tinted windows, scratch on the right rear bumper. I was considering snapping a picture of the license plate when Gypsy began to growl, and as I turned to see what she was growling at, a man in a black jacket emerged from the walkway between the lilacs. I had rehearsed this scenario in my head a thousand times, determined it wouldn't play out like it did in my nightmares, yet I stood paralyzed. Gypsy lunged, yanking the slack out of the leash and knocking the Mace and the phone from my hands. I scurried backward, dragging her with me, a scream rising in my throat.

"Sarah?" the man said. "It's Nick Farrow. I'm sorry—I didn't mean to startle you. I was just checking to see if you were home." He held up an ID. "We spoke on the phone?"

I steadied myself, my chest heaving, trying to catch my breath. I told Gypsy to sit. A growl simmered in her throat, but she obeyed. I examined the ID closely enough to be sure it was real, compared the picture to the face in front of me. Over the phone, I'd imagined him grizzled and paunchy like Sheriff Krieger, but Farrow was closer to my age, maybe late twenties, with the athletic bearing of a runner, all long limbs and energy. He had dark hair and greenish eyes and an apologetic half smile that might have been endearing if he hadn't just popped out of the bushes and scared the crap out of me. He probably used the same expression on girls at bars and had a bit of luck.

He bent down to retrieve my Mace and phone and gave them back to me. "Hey, there," he said to Gypsy, extending a hand for her to sniff.

"She doesn't like men." The words were barely out of my mouth before Gypsy went for his hand, but instead of biting, she tentatively licked him.

Farrow smiled at me, a dimple piercing his cheek. I didn't smile back. We both knew he hadn't come to make friends.

"You can't just show up at my house," I said. "I haven't done anything."

"Of course," he said. "I apologize. I was in the area, so I thought I'd check in. See if you'd had a chance to consider my request." He took a square of paper from his pocket, unfolded it, and handed it to me. "This is Abby," he said.

The girl looked younger than sixteen, small and bird boned, though maybe the picture wasn't recent. She wore a baggy white polo shirt and long navy skirt, her expression blank, mouth clamped shut, hair forced into a tight bun. The photo was poorly lit and slightly out of focus, not the sort of image parents usually chose to represent a missing child. Handwritten notes at the bottom stated that she had brown hair, brown eyes, no identifying marks.

"I tried to look her up," I said. "I couldn't find anything."

"Not every missing kid makes the news," he said. "As I'm sure you know. Some cases attract more media attention than others." He scanned the street, turned back to me. "Do you have time to sit and talk for a minute? We could go to the coffee shop down the block, if you'd be more comfortable."

"Here's fine," I said. "But it has to be quick, I have to get ready for work."

He followed me through the lilac hedge and we sat on the steps. Gypsy busied herself slurping all the water out of the birdbath.

"I thought of you when I started looking for Abby," he said. "I remembered seeing you in the paper."

"Yeah. You said on the phone that she's like me. What did you mean by that?"

"Well, on the surface, there are quite a few similarities. She's from a rural area, like you, a few hours from Wisteria. Similar age at the time of disappearance. She's homeschooled, family's deeply religious."

"You said before that you were sure she was taken, even though you couldn't rule out the possibility that she ran away. What makes you think so?"

He crossed his arms over his chest. His jacket bunched, and I wondered if he had a gun concealed beneath it.

"Her parents thought she left on her own because they'd been arguing over her behavior. She didn't want to follow their rules. They said she'd always been a difficult kid. Rebellious. But she's not equipped to manage on her own. No street smarts. No money. No ID. No phone."

"And? That's it? You think nobody runs away unprepared?"

He eyed me carefully. "She has other family out there. People she could have turned to. She hasn't been in contact with anyone. I think if she took off on her own, she would have gone to someone who could help her."

"And you really think it could be the same guy, the one who took me?"

"Yes. I think it's a possibility."

"Even though it's been five years?" It was one of the things the sheriff had mentioned in the paper, casting doubt on my story. *There would be other abductions. A guy who could do something like this and get away with it, it wouldn't be his first time or his last. There'd be others and we haven't seen any indication that there are.* My parents hadn't brought any newspapers into the house, though I'd read some of the articles later, online. *Have you ever seen anything like that, where somebody was kidnapped and let go a week later?* Sheriff Krieger had said. *In thirty-odd years of law enforcement, I can tell you that I haven't. Doesn't pass the smell test, does it?*

"Sheriff Krieger said . . ." I stopped myself, not wanting to give voice to his other concerns.

"Sheriff Krieger isn't what I would call an expert," he said. A jab at the sheriff. Nice touch. Nick Farrow had clearly mastered the art of Good Cop. "There are plenty of reasons why you wouldn't see a person committing other crimes for a period of time," he continued. "The most obvious, they move away, get sick or die, go to prison for something else. It's possible he might have needed some time to regroup, or he was trying not to do it again. Or, how about this: What if it hasn't been five years? Maybe there were other disappearances that didn't get reported, or maybe they were reported but no one noticed a pattern. Maybe he's still taking girls, but he's not letting them go."

Something flickered in my chest, and I tamped it down. Farrow was merely speculating. He had no proof of anything.

"The way you were interrogated . . . I know it must have been difficult. Your account was—"

"Unbelievable. That's what they called it." Over and over, throughout hours of questioning in which my answers were twisted and picked apart. There were accusations and insinuations, a palpable disbelief of my version of events, despite the marks on my body and the ghoulish, unrecognizable reflection I saw in the bathroom mirror at the station. By the end, the thing I wanted most was to get out of there, away from them. It didn't matter anymore what my story was or whether they believed it.

"That's not what I was going to say."

Gypsy flopped down on the ground at my feet, her dripping snout resting on my shoe, her eyes on Farrow.

"Sarah," he said. "I believe you. And I believe that you can help me—that you can help Abby. I know this can't be easy for you, but all I want is to hear your story from *you*, not filtered through Sheriff Krieger or a tabloid reporter or anyone else. That's all. What do you think?"

"It's not that I don't *want* to help, but . . . if you believe me, if you've been through the file, you know I don't have any idea who did this. I never saw his face, never saw where he took me. I was blindfolded and kept in the dark the entire time. That's the truth. I told the detectives everything, and it didn't do any good."

"Their minds were made up from the start. They could have missed crucial details. You might remember something that didn't seem significant then but could make all the difference now."

I fidgeted with the piece of paper, a flimsy and inadequate stand-in for a flesh-and-blood girl. My fingernails carved a frame around Abby's face. She was a phantom made of ink. I could cover her with my palm and she would cease to exist.

"Look, you don't know me. I know I'm asking a lot when I ask you to trust me. I don't blame you for not wanting to revisit a horribly traumatic experience. But the person who did this to you might still be out there, preying on other girls. I want to find him and put him away, and I'll do whatever it takes. Even if I'm wrong and there's no connection, I promise that I'll do everything I can to resolve your case, too, whether you decide to help me or not. You didn't have anyone fighting for you then, but you do now. And I know you'd want the same for Abby, for her to have all the help she can get."

He was good at this. Passionate, persuasive, sincere. If he'd been running for office, I would have voted for him. I refolded the paper so I wouldn't have to look at Abby's face. She was sixteen. Sylvie's age. "I have to get ready for work."

He turned to look at me dead-on. "Abby's been missing for twenty-four days. Sixteen more days than you. She could be running out of time. Or maybe she already has. Either way, I need to find her. All I want is to talk to you. Ask a few questions. Fill in some gaps."

He didn't accuse me of being selfish or cowardly, not in so many words. He was more subtle than Sheriff Krieger. He remained calm, his voice steady, his hands perfectly still, but as he held my gaze, his eyes revealed something else. Desperation. How many dead ends had he reached to wind up here with me? What mental contortions had been necessary to convince himself that I possessed a hidden key, that if I would just talk to him, he'd be able to unlock the mystery?

I tried to believe, for a moment, that he was right, that I could help find this missing girl. What would happen if I exhumed Sarabeth, crawled back inside her skin? The interview room at the station in Wisteria flashed into my mind. The fluorescent lights, the orange plastic chairs, the sickening smell of Sheriff Krieger's wintergreen chewing tobacco. My throat constricted, threatening to choke me. I reminded myself that I was safe, that I was not the one trapped in the dark. I clamped my hands onto the edge of the concrete step, drew in a breath for four counts, held it another four, blew it out.

"I'm sorry, I don't think I can."

He tried to keep the disappointment from showing on his face. Or maybe it was anger. "I get it," he said. "I do." He handed me a card with his phone number. "But please, at least think about it. Sleep on it. Call me if you change your mind?"

"Sure." The word wisped out, a ghost on my lips, already threatening to haunt me. I wished I'd said no and been done with it.

The girl's face loomed in my mind as I showered and dressed. I hoped that she was okay, that Farrow was wrong and she was fine, because there was nothing I could do to help her. I didn't want to relive my abduction. Just talking to Farrow for a few minutes had stirred everything up, and it felt like a swarm of ants were chittering beneath my skin. I wished that I hadn't sworn off my anxiety pills, or that I'd at least been smart enough to save an emergency stash for something like this. I wanted to forget about Abby. I didn't want to think of her chained in that dark hole for twenty-four days. It was hard enough living with Sarabeth's ghost. I didn't need Abby Donnelly's moving into my head with her.

# CHAPTER 4

# SARABETH, THEN

## AGE 14

Thursday became my favorite day, the day I baked for the Darlings. I'd arrive after breakfast, the kitchen smelling of bacon grease, coffee percolating on the stove. Mr. Darling would take a few minutes to chat with me about the calves or the weather before heading back out to the barn, while Mrs. Darling cleaned the cast iron skillet and put away the breakfast dishes. Mrs. Darling would then retire to the sitting room with her *Daily Guideposts* devotional, turn on the TV, and drift into a late-morning nap until *The Young and the Restless* came on.

When Tom was done with his chores, he'd sit at the kitchen table with a stack of workbooks he was supposed to complete so he wouldn't fall behind over the summer like he had the year before. He spent more time talking than working. He confided that he'd failed nearly every subject after his dad died, and he'd had to repeat eighth grade while his friends moved on to high school and left him behind. I could sympathize. I hated thinking of my old friends together, without me, at Wisteria High.

The last Thursday in August, Tom was waiting for me at the

kitchen table, his arm buried up to the elbow in a box of Cap'n Crunch. "I'm supposed to tell you sorry, Gramma forgot to let you know they'd be gone." He extracted a handful of cereal, yellow sugar dust clinging to his skin.

"Gone?"

"They go to Springfield the last Thursday of the month to see Gramma's cousin in the nursing home. After that, they eat lunch and go to Sam's Club and the craft store and sometimes Gramma's arthritis doctor. They won't be back till suppertime."

"Oh," I said, trying not to sound disappointed. "I guess I should go."

"What?" he said. "Why?"

I was thinking that my parents wouldn't want me hanging around with a boy all day, unsupervised, even if it was Tom Darling, but that obviously hadn't occurred to him, and maybe it hadn't occurred to Mr. and Mrs. Darling either.

"Did your grandma say anything? Did she still want me to work today?"

"Yeah. She asked if you could do half the oatmeal cookies with raisins, half without."

"Sure, whatever you want." I opened the cabinet to get out the flour and sugar.

"I already finished my chores," Tom said, grinning. His teeth were too big for his mouth, his lips barely able to close over them. "I can help you with the baking, and then we'll get done quicker and have time to do other stuff before they get back."

I leaned against the counter. "What do you mean? What other stuff?"

"I dunno. Whatever you want. Watch TV? Play videogames? I've got a computer up in my room."

I tried not to react, hoping my face didn't reveal just how

badly I wanted to get on the internet. Maybe he was testing me, trying to get me into trouble. "My parents have rules about that kind of thing," I said carefully.

"I know," he said. "I won't tell."

"What makes you think I *want* to do those things?"

"Why wouldn't you?" he said.

I stared at him, all teeth and gawky limbs. There were cereal crumbs at the corners of his mouth. He was looking at me funny not because I was dressed like a pioneer, but because I had suggested that I didn't want to watch TV. Somehow, he'd seen right through the pretend me and glimpsed the real me underneath. I started laughing, and his grin widened until he was laughing, too.

We turned the TV up in the den so we could hear the morning talk shows and Tom mixed cookie dough while I made the bread. The first batch of cookies burned while we were upstairs watching YouTube videos and didn't hear the timer go off. I panicked at the veil of smoke in the kitchen, imagining what my mother would say if she found out I'd been careless enough to set fire to the Darlings' oven.

"No big deal," Tom said, fanning at the smoke with a dish towel. "We'll just make more. But we should get rid of the evidence." He scraped the burnt cookies into a bag and we took them out to the barn. Mr. Darling's workbench sat in one corner, and an assortment of old livestock tools hung from a pegboard on the wall above it. He'd explained to Eli and me what they were used for one day. There was a pair of long-handled castration pliers, a poultry hook, a metal syringe with a pistol grip for administering vaccinations, an ear tagger that resembled a hole punch, but with a sharp spike on one side to pierce through flesh. Tom picked through oversized shears and rusted clamps until he found what he was looking for: a slingshot.

"My dad's," he said. "He used to hunt squirrels with it. Tried to teach me, but I'm no good at moving targets. We'd go down and launch rocks at the pond, see who could get one out the farthest. He could shoot all the way across if he wanted, never even hit the water. But he'd let me beat him sometimes."

"So . . . we're gonna slingshot the cookies into the pond?"

"Yeah," he said. "I mean, we could just throw 'em away but I thought this'd be more fun. We can take the Gator. Just don't tell Grampa I got it out when he wasn't here."

"Anything that happens on Secret Thursday stays between us," I said.

"The first rule of Secret Thursday is you don't talk about Secret Thursday."

"Okay."

"It's from a movie," he said. "Never mind. Let's shake on it."

He squeezed my hand tight, and I instinctively looked around to make sure no one was in the shadows of the barn to see. Mama said that secrets were like bruises in an apple, hidden beneath the skin, brown worm tracks tunneling down to the core and rotting you from within. *What's done in darkness*, she warned, *shall come to light*, and she'd done her best to prove it. She had ferreted out and disposed of the Maybelline lip gloss I'd stashed in my mattress, the E. E. Cummings poem I'd torn from a school library book and folded into my Bible, an old valentine from Jack tucked into the back of my underwear drawer. Each loss left me emptier and stoked flames of resentment toward my mother. Secrets were the only contraband I had left, and that made them all the more exciting. On the scale of secrets, this one was small, but it hummed with electric warmth, burning bright in the hidden hollows of my heart.

# CHAPTER 5

# SARAH, NOW

I woke to darkness, my pulse stabbing with the rapid insistence of a sewing machine needle. The phone was ringing, but lingering in my ears was the unmistakable sound of scissors slicing through the dark, the metal blades grinding against each other. A nightmare. I lay paralyzed, scanning the room for unfamiliar shadows. *Breathe in, one, two, three, four, hold, one, two, three, four. Breathe out.* I was surprised I'd slept at all, Abby's face appearing every time I closed my eyes.

Downstairs, Gypsy started to bark. The phone was still ringing, or had stopped and started again, an annoying jangly tune reserved for calls, not alarms. Helen was the only one who ever called, and she only called in the night if something went wrong and she needed the emergency vet.

I swiped to answer and Farrow's voice boomed in my ear. "Sarah, it's Nick Farrow."

"Nick." I said it aloud, the single syllable sticking in my dry mouth.

"I apologize if I woke you, but something's come up. Another girl's gone missing. From Lone Ridge, south of St. Louis. We don't know enough yet to be sure, but there are definite similarities."

*Another girl?* My throat was raw, like I'd been screaming in my sleep. I tried to swallow.

"I wanted to do this on your terms," he continued. "Give you a chance to get used to the idea, let you come to the decision on your own. And I think you would have, in time. But right now we need to throw everything we've got at this case. It can't wait."

"What are you saying? You're going to force me to . . . do what, exactly?"

"Not force," he said. "I know you want to help—I could tell when you saw Abby's picture. I need to interview you today. Now. I know you want to put this behind you for good, and I don't want to cause you any more grief, but if you won't talk to me, I'll have to bring your case back into the spotlight. Put it out to the media as the five-year anniversary of your unsolved abduction, stir up interest, hopefully drum up some witnesses, leads, suspects. Get everyone talking about it again. People might find you, figure out who you are." He paused to let it sink in. "I don't want that and I know you don't either. But I need some insight into your case, and I have to get it somehow. I'd much rather get it straight from you."

I was fully awake now. "This feels like a threat. Like blackmail."

"It's a choice," he said. "I'm doing my job, and these missing girls are my number-one priority. I'll do whatever it takes to find them."

He had me cornered and he knew it. Talk to him in private or have reporters at my door. It wasn't much of a choice.

"I'm not Sheriff Krieger," he said. "This is different. You're afraid it won't do anything but reopen old wounds. That it won't help. But what if it does?"

I hadn't wanted to relive what had happened to me, but it was already too late for that. The nightmares were back, my anxiety flaring. He wasn't going to give up. I could do it and get it over with. Tell my side of the story. Haul Sarabeth out of her shallow grave and then shovel her right back in again. When Abby appeared in my dreams, I could tell her that I'd tried.

"I don't do interview rooms. None of those mirrored windows or cameras or closed doors. No police stations."

"No problem," he said. "We can take a drive."

"Why can't we talk on the phone, like we're doing now?" I knew he wouldn't settle for that. He wasn't Sheriff Krieger, but he was still a cop. He'd want to see if I'd pick at my fingernails, if my eyes would dart. He'd read my expression and body language and decide if I was telling the truth, if I had something to hide. Sheriff Krieger had remarked, at various points in my hours-long interview, how odd it was that I hadn't cried. *Never seen anything like it. What you just went through, not a single tear. I've seen girls bawl over a traffic ticket.*

"I thought you could come with me to Lone Ridge," he said. "And just . . . observe. Look, listen, see if anything stands out."

I couldn't believe what he was saying. "You want to take me along to a crime scene? You're really asking me that?"

"It's not a crime scene. It's a girl's home. A girl like you. Who's gone missing. I want to get your perspective. That's all."

"Is that even allowed? Because it doesn't seem like it would be. Did your boss sign off on it?"

"It's unorthodox, maybe. But two girls are missing, there's not much to go on, and you might be our best chance to crack this open."

He'd slithered around my questions without a real answer. "Let's say you're right, and the cases are connected. What happens if he's there? What if I don't recognize him but he recognizes me?"

"I'll be with you the entire time. You'll be surrounded by law enforcement. If anyone's acting strange, we'll be right on top of it."

Every alarm in my body was going off, warning me that it was a bad idea, that nothing good would come of it. But two things kept me from saying no. One was the thought of the girls, alone in the dark. The other was the feeling, five years later, that I was still chained to that wall. Therapy and medication hadn't made it go away, and I didn't know what would. Farrow was right. *You're afraid it won't help. But what if it does?* This was a chance to do something. Maybe it wouldn't make a difference, but maybe it would. I wanted to try. Somewhere inside me, Sarabeth was clawing her way back into the daylight.

"It's one day, Sarah. That's all I'm asking. I'll have you back tonight."

I pulled the phone away to check the time. It was a quarter to seven, not the middle of the night like I'd first thought. Beyond the curtains, sunlight would be creeping up from the horizon.

"I just woke up."

"Coffee, then." He was five steps ahead of me. "I'll grab some on the way to pick you up."

"Wait. If I do this . . . if I tell you everything I know and do everything I can to help today, and nothing comes of it, do you swear that'll be the end of it? You'll stop calling and showing up at my house and leave me alone?"

"Yes." He paused. "You have my word."

I got out of bed and switched on the light. "We'll have to drop off my dog on the way."

"You got it," he said. "Be there in ten."

I felt light-headed, almost dizzy. I wondered if he was already at the coffee shop down the street, the order placed before I'd even agreed. He hadn't bothered to ask what I wanted. I half suspected that if I looked out the window, he'd be at the curb, waiting.

Helen had answered my text right away, happy to keep Gypsy for the day since I didn't know what time I'd get back. She glanced at Farrow waiting in the Tahoe, raised her eyebrows at me. "No plans for the weekend, huh?"

"It . . . just came up," I said, my ears burning. "Last minute."

"Mm-hm." She laughed and shook her head. "I'm just messing with you. It's none of my business. Though I am more than willing to lend an ear if you want to tell me all about it later." She touched my arm and leaned in, like a girlfriend would. "You have a good time." Helen waved as we pulled away, her fingers fluttering.

Though Gypsy had only been in the vehicle for a matter of minutes, she'd managed to leave hair on the dash, the seats, my clothes. I brushed it away as best I could, watched it float through the air. Aside from the fur, Farrow's car was impeccably clean. The radio was tuned to a news station, but he'd turned the volume down too low to make out the words.

"Thank you," he said, not looking away from the road. "For doing this." I studied his profile, the tension in his jaw. His hands clamped the steering wheel tight enough to squeeze the blood from his fingers. He took the ramp onto the interstate and continued to accelerate, slipping past a row of semis.

"The girl from Lone Ridge," I said. "What's her name?"

"Destiny Jewell," he said. "She's fourteen. Lives on a farm out in the boonies with her mom. Homeschooled. Been missing for two days. They're searching the woods and surrounding area but haven't found anything yet."

We drove past the strip malls and fast-food restaurants of the outer suburbs, the twisting spines of roller coasters at the Six Flags amusement park rising out of the trees in the distance. I liked living near the city, insulated by the trappings of civilization, surrounded by strangers. It made me feel safe, which was absurd; the murder rate in St. Louis was the worst in the state, and I barely interacted with my neighbors. Still, my stomach knotted with the knowledge that I was leaving the protective cocoon I'd hidden inside for the past five years. I wasn't ready, but maybe I never would be.

It was unsettling how quickly signs of life faded away as we sped south, businesses and apartment complexes replaced first by fields and then rolling hills and then craggy cliffs where the road had been blasted out of solid rock. The same rugged, breathtaking scenery you'd see in a horror movie before a young woman takes the wrong shortcut. So many acres of isolation, of nothingness. There were still plenty of places for people to disappear.

"So," Farrow said, fingers tapping on the steering wheel. "You like your job at the shelter?"

"You don't have to do that," I said. "Make small talk. Just ask what you want to ask and get it over with. That's why I'm here."

"All right," he said, glancing in the rearview mirror and then clicking on the cruise control. "So you were taken by a man wearing a mask, and you woke up blindfolded. You were blind-folded until he let you go and kept in the dark. You don't know how far you drove, you never saw anything inside or outside the place you were held, and you never saw the face of the person who kept you there."

"Correct."

"The medical exam revealed multiple injuries—bruising and wounds consistent with restraints, a bloody nose, contusions on the head and face, lacerations on your hands, and another bleed-ing wound on your hip. Your hair had been cut. But there was no exam for sexual assault. According to your interview, you claimed you were not sexually assaulted and declined to be examined. Is that correct?"

"Yes." I thought of the nurse who tended to me, how she wiped off the dried blood, kept my body covered as much as she could with a paper sheet. She apologized for the bright lights, avoided looking me in the eye.

"I told you that I believe you, and I do. I don't want you to take this as an attack on your credibility, I just want to make sure that we have all the right information. Given the nature of your family's religious background . . . it would be understandable if you didn't feel comfortable discussing that sort of thing with the detectives when they questioned you back then. I'm aware of the stigma in certain communities, how women are made to feel that they're tainted somehow, and they want to avoid that. If any-thing happened that you were afraid for your parents or people in the community to find out, you can tell me now—they don't need to know. It could be relevant to the case."

"I wasn't raped," I said, the word ringing like a church bell. That had been a difficult thing for the sheriff to believe—if a man had abducted me, wouldn't he have raped me? Why else would someone want to steal a teenage girl? In the end it didn't matter what I said, people would think what they wanted.

"Okay," Farrow said. "Then let's move on." He swerved around a shredded tire, the Tahoe vibrating as he crossed the caution strip. "I've read through your file I don't know how many times, and the one thing I can't figure out is probably the most important part of the puzzle. The motive. If you want to catch someone like this, it helps to know why they're doing it, what they want. Did you get any hint of what he wanted from you? Some larger plan?"

"I don't know. I mean, when I think about it now . . . it was almost like I was being prepared for something that never happened. Maybe he just hadn't gotten around to whatever he was going to do."

"If that's the case, what was he waiting for? It makes me think you might have been the first, that he hadn't quite worked everything out yet. But I also wonder if there was a personal connection . . . if he knew you, and that made him reluctant to follow through."

His phone buzzed and he checked the screen, sighed, put it back down.

"All right, how about suspects. In your interview, you mentioned some young men from town, former classmates. This part's a bit messy, but from what I could tell, they had alibis for the day you went missing . . . supposedly they went to a basketball game together. I don't know how thoroughly that was checked out. One of them claimed that you'd told him you were going to run away, which Sheriff Krieger repeated in the newspaper, though the guy later claimed he hadn't spoken to you. Do you think they might have been involved?"

"I don't know," I said. "They'd come by the farm stand sometimes and make stupid jokes. Thought it was funny to mess with me. But I don't know if one of them could've pulled off something like that." I hadn't given Jack's name. Only the others. I didn't like to think of Jack having anything to do with it.

"Maybe worth another look," he said. "You used a neighbor's internet from time to time. Did you have any online relationships you didn't tell the police about?"

"I did a homeschool course online. My parents knew. I wasn't allowed to use social media or anything like that."

"But did you?"

"No." The instinct was still there, to deny anything my parents would have disapproved of. "I mean, I looked at it. Tom—the Darlings' grandson, it was his computer—he had accounts, but I never had one of my own. I'd look things up sometimes, maybe things my parents wouldn't have liked, but I didn't talk to anyone."

"When you came back, did you notice anyone acting strangely toward you? Anyone change their behavior?"

"I didn't have a chance to notice anything, really. I was kept at home after, until I left town. My family acted different around me, but I couldn't blame them. They were worried about keeping reporters out, trying to pretend things would go back to normal."

Outside the window, the scenery was unfamiliar. I hadn't looked Lone Ridge up on the map. "How far south of St. Louis are we going?" I asked.

"About four hours," he said. "A hundred miles from Wisteria."

I gritted my teeth, feeling like I might puke. A hundred miles from home. Farrow was using the same strategy my counselor had employed to help me adjust to my new life. Baby steps. *Just talk to me,* he'd said. *In the car. On the way to a crime scene. In the Ozarks.* I didn't want to guess what the next step might be, but it was too late to turn back now.

Farrow kept on with his questions, trying to extract something new out of the well-worn details of my file as we drove deeper into the Ozarks and entered the Mark Twain National Forest. He didn't circle back to sex, didn't obsess over the parts the sheriff had, how I had been undressed, bathed. I answered everything, keeping my eyes on the scenery to ground myself in the present. We passed a mobile home with a blue tarp on the roof and a yard full of battered Christmas decorations, an abandoned gas station with a Confederate flag hanging over the broken pumps. Buzzards gathered for the plentiful roadkill, gorging until we were nearly on top of them, their wide black wings swooping over the windshield.

"I'm working on getting the blood evidence from the nightgown retested," Farrow said.

"They called it a nightgown in the news, but it was a slip, actually. Not that it matters. You can't retest it because the sheriff's office misplaced it. Or they threw it out when the evidence room flooded. Or it got stolen when a tweaker broke in to get his meth back. Those were some of the answers my lawyer got."

"Huh," he said. "They might have lost the slip, but there were extensive bloodstains, and multiple samples were cut out to send to the lab. Those are still intact. I know you thought there was a chance there might have been some of his blood on you, and since some of the tests were inconclusive, I thought it was worth checking, see if they missed something."

"Inconclusive? What does that mean? I don't remember anybody saying that."

"It might not have been mentioned if it wasn't deemed im-

portant. Could mean lots of things. Maybe the sample was con-
taminated. Maybe not enough material to get an accurate result.
There might be some different methods we can try, though."

"Why didn't anybody tell me we could redo the tests? When
they said the slip was gone, I thought there was nothing left,
nothing I could do."

"I don't know," he said. "Miscommunication? Incompe-
tence? Omission? Whoever it was probably didn't know about
the samples. Sometimes it seems like things are swept under the
rug, but usually it's just simple human error. I know that probably doesn't make you feel any better about it. It certainly doesn't
make it okay."

The original analysis had identified no DNA but my own.
The slip was all I had; the nurse had rinsed the blood from my
hands without stopping to consider that it might be evidence. I'd
thought that if they found his blood, it would prove that I was
telling the truth. Sheriff Krieger hadn't believed me when I told
him what happened the night I was dumped alongside the highway. I was far from Wisteria when the results came back, but I
didn't need to see him face-to-face to hear his mocking voice in
my head. *All that blood, it's all yours. You can see why nobody
believes you, Sarabeth. Your story just doesn't add up.*

# CHAPTER 6

# SARABETH, THEN

## AGE 16

There were footsteps overhead, muddled voices, but Retta and I were alone in the church basement. We had volunteered to stay and clean up after the youth group meeting—or rather, Retta had volunteered us both. She hummed a hymn as she wiped down the folding tables, a soft smile on her face while she worked. She was the embodiment of everything we were taught to be—obedient, pleasing, modest, devout—but she still liked to gossip, unlike most of the other girls, who chatted about things like homemade laundry detergent as though it were actually interesting, even when their mothers weren't right there, listening. I could say things to Retta that I couldn't say to anyone else. We kept each other's secrets.

"Pastor Rick was filled with the spirit tonight, wasn't he?" Retta said.

"I guess."

I hadn't heard anything the pastor said. I'd been too focused on his son, Noah, who'd been seated at the boys' table because boys and girls weren't allowed to sit together at youth group.

Noah had black hair that gleamed under the fluorescent lights and eyes the faded blue of my favorite jean jacket, the one my mother had given to the Salvation Army. He was built like a bull, blocky and lumbering, but he had a quiet, gentle manner and wore old-fashioned suspenders, which enhanced a vague resemblance to my very first crush, Albert Ingalls from *Little House on the Prairie*. In my fantasies, Noah was a bookish football player who would take me on dates to Dairy Queen or the skating rink and then make out with me in the parking lot, in a car with the radio playing.

Apart from the fantasies, my relationship with Noah consisted mostly of furtive glances and wistful stares. We would gaze at each other, lips parting, blood rushing to stain our cheeks. We were never completely alone—social interactions between boys and girls were carefully monitored and controlled by the adults at church—but whenever we were allowed to mingle, we would gravitate toward each other. If he saw me gathering hymnals or moving tables, he would come help. One evening, while stacking chairs, his hand had touched mine and lingered. We'd stood there breathless for a long moment, the air crackling between us.

Tonight, he had stared at the table with a vacant expression while his father railed about sin and salvation, and I wondered if he tuned out Pastor Rick like I did, if he was thinking about other things, like sex, or his father suffering a horrible accident that would somehow sever his vocal cords and render him mute. Noah had looked up and caught me watching him. Neither of us looked away. Pink crept up his neck, above his collar, and finally he looked back down at the table, at the greasy bag of popcorn that had made the rounds and come to him last. He hadn't touched it. There was probably nothing left but hard, unopened kernels in the bottom, what my father called old maids.

"I saw you and Noah," Retta giggle-whispered.

"What?" I knelt to scoop a piece of smashed popcorn off the concrete floor.

"I saw the way he was looking at you. And he was *blushing*."

"He blushes all the time. At everything. He blushed when his dad called on him."

Pastor Rick had asked what it meant to be an evangelical at Holy Rock and, ignoring the flurry of raised hands, called on his son. *We have to spread the word of God, of salvation, to everyone we can, to save as many souls as possible,* Noah recited in his soft monotone. *Or the burden of their lost souls in Hell rests upon us.*

"True," Retta said. "But I've never seen him look at anybody else like that. I think he really likes you."

I tried not to smile. While Retta would never admit to having a crush on anyone, herself—she wanted to save those feelings for her future husband—she was always eager to talk about courtship and marriage.

"Can you imagine, marrying a preacher's son?" she squealed. "That would be such a blessing for your family."

I made a face. Marrying into the Blackburn family was not part of my fantasy. I was fairly certain I would strangle Pastor Rick if I had to spend any more time listening to him than I already did. His wife, Minnie, was even more fanatical than he was, if such a thing was possible. She was sturdy like Noah, but her pale skin, large, unblinking eyes, and puckered mouth made her look like a haunted Victorian doll. She had suffered a series of miscarriages after Noah was born, but she fervently believed that every single thing that happened, good or bad, was God's will, that all suffering had purpose. She endeavored to make herself worthy through faith and prayer, and she left it in His hands to one day reveal His plan.

I couldn't imagine the purpose of such divine cruelty, allowing her to conceive over and over but never bear a child, especially as the wife of a pastor in a church full of children, but her strength and steadfastness were admired by the entire congregation. If Holy Rock allowed for saints or idols, they would have erected a statue of Minnie Blackburn.

"It doesn't matter if we like each other. Pastor Rick would never approve." I'd earned a permanent spot on the pastor's bad list soon after our arrival at Holy Rock. The youth group was charged with cleaning up the graveyard at the edge of the woods behind the church. Mama hadn't yet sewn proper dresses for me, so I was wearing someone else's castoff. It was too big and made of heavy wool, better suited for winter. I got hot pulling weeds and scrubbing stones, so I snuck away to dip my feet in the creek. I slipped on the rocks and drenched my dress and decided to take it off to dry. I lay in the sun in the tank top and shorts I'd been wearing in place of a slip, the dress draped over a branch, while the other kids finished their work. When I opened my eyes, Pastor Rick was casting a shadow over me, the rest of the youth group behind him. Most of the boys either tried to avoid looking at me or zeroed in on the bits of exposed flesh like they'd never seen arms and legs before. I knew I was in trouble, but the look on the pastor's face sent me into a fit of nervous laughter. It was the first time I really noticed Noah. He was the only one looking me in the eye, his face pink, trying not to laugh. I felt an instant kinship with him, the two of us sharing a joke no one else found funny.

There were other incidents at church, early on—singing inappropriate radio songs to the children when I helped out in the preschool room, shouting a curse word when I stubbed my toe on a pew, failing to complete my Sunday school lessons. I was never intentionally bad, but my normal behavior didn't come close to meeting the Blackburns' standards.

"You've changed," Retta said. "Grown up." It wasn't so much that I'd changed, but that I'd learned how to behave to best avoid punishment. I had enough scars across the back of my thighs from my father's belt. "And you should give the pastor some credit," Retta continued. "He's kind. Understanding. Forgiving."

Retta idolized Pastor Rick. He had guided her through the darkest time of her life, something that no one else knew about aside from Retta's family and me. She had whispered her story one afternoon while we played dolls, as she laid them together in the shoebox bed in their wedding clothes.

Retta had older half brothers, her father's sons from his late first wife. When she was little, one of the brothers, Leon, would come into her room at night and wake her up to play. She had liked the attention at first, the shared secret. But she didn't like some of the games or the way he made her play them. She started to have a stomachache every day and would burst into tears over little things. Her mother heard a noise one night and went to check on her and caught Leon slipping out of Retta's room. The next morning at breakfast, there were two empty seats at the table. Retta's mother explained that her father and stepbrother had left for a weekend prayer retreat, and breakfast continued as usual.

Very little was said in the family about what had happened. Leon confessed his sins and was forgiven. He married soon after and moved to his wife's family farm outside of town, but the families still sat together at church like normal and gathered every Sunday night for supper.

Retta's parents never spoke of the incident again, and when Retta grew sullen, they sent her to Pastor Rick for counseling. He prayed with her, but no matter how much she prayed, she couldn't get rid of the unpleasant thoughts, so Pastor Rick tried various other therapies. When she was hesitant to say things aloud, he urged her to act them out or write them down. She wrote her secrets on scraps of paper and stuffed them in a canning jar under her bed, but they kept her awake at night, and she feared her mother would find them. Pastor Rick had suggested she burn them, but she thought it best to keep them contained, hidden away where they couldn't be found, so she buried the jar in her backyard just outside the fence where the sweet autumn clematis grew. One jar, and then another, until she had emptied herself out and her secret garden was sown.

She said she no longer thought about the bad things that had happened. But I did, sometimes. I'd see Leon at church and imagine the secrets buried in the earth like seeds, waiting to sprout and grow toward the light. I wondered what dark flowers would bloom on the twisted vines.

Retta and I were almost done cleaning when we heard footsteps coming down the stairs. Noah appeared, and Retta made big eyes at me.

"Hello, Noah," she said. "Can we help you with something?"

"I just need to take a few chairs upstairs," he said.

"I'll help," Retta said. "We were just finishing up." She gave my arm a quick squeeze, grabbed a folding chair from the closet, and hurried up the stairs.

Noah and I stood staring at each other. We were alone, though not for long. I inched toward him, closing the distance between us, not sure what to say. I wanted to ask him a thousand things, to hear the words that waited on his tongue, unspoken, every time our eyes met across a room. I wanted to know if he thought of me the same way that I thought about him.

"You looked . . . distracted, earlier," I said. "What were you thinking about?"

"The salvation game," he said.

"Oh," I said, deflated. He'd been paying attention to the lesson after all. Pastor Rick made us play the salvation game each summer at Bible camp. One person was "it" and had to chase the rest of us through the field behind the church, tagging kids to "save" them, and the saved would in turn try to tag others. Anyone who got tagged would go to Heaven, while those who made it across the field were condemned to Hell. It was a dumb game, but we were supposed to take it seriously, a real-life battle for souls. My little sister, Sylvie, wept and prayed for those she failed to save.

"Remember last time? When we were the only two left."

"Yes," I said. I remembered. Noah and I had been sprinting toward the woods, racing, my long skirt gathered in my hands to keep me from tripping. I'd glanced over my shoulder at Sylvie, who was trailing behind us, and Noah had slowed down to let her catch him.

"I was thinking," he said. "What if we just kept running?"

"Sarabeth! Time to go!" Mama called from above, her voice sharp as an axe. Noah gave me a mournful smile and grabbed the chairs he'd come for. As we climbed the stairs under my mother's watchful eye, I imagined us running for the woods, not stopping, never looking back.

# CHAPTER 7

# SARAH, NOW

I had forgotten how steep the hills were, how the top of each one looked like the end of the road because you couldn't see the drop on the other side. I clung to the armrest, my stomach lurching as we plunged down into gullies and barreled around hairpin curves. The homesteads we passed were scattered far from any neighbors, decrepit trailers and motor homes, sagging shacks with the roofs caved in, timeworn outhouses clinging to the edges of ravines, skeletonized cars rusting beneath shrouds of dead vines. Even the houses that appeared uninhabitable showed evidence of life: mums planted in a broken toilet in the front yard, laundry hanging out to dry. We saw a few signs for towns that no longer existed, what Daddy would call a wide spot in the road. Cell service evaporated and we pulled over at the edge of a dry creek bed to check the paper map.

"We must be right about here." Farrow's finger hovered over an expanse of green. "We've crossed into the Irish Wilderness but haven't hit the Eleven Point River." He steered the Tahoe back onto the pavement and we rode in silence for a few more miles. "I think this is it," he said finally, flicking the blinker as we approached an unmarked dirt road. The only clue that anyone might live at the end of it was a mangled mailbox lying in the ditch.

A tunnel of trees closed around us, blocking out the sun and momentarily rendering us blind. The SUV lurched uphill over rocks and potholes, brush scraping against the doors. Two miles on we emerged back into the sunlight at a hilltop farm consisting of a ragtag collection of weathered buildings with rusted tin roofs, a dilapidated camper, and a graveyard of tires and tractor parts. A bonfire burned in a stony field hemmed by barbed wire.

We parked next to a police cruiser. The view through the windshield was extraordinary—the earth falling away beyond the fence into a wooded ravine, endless hills fading into the distance like receding waves. The expansive vista somehow made me feel claustrophobic, like the sky was closing in on me. It looked so much like home.

Farrow reached into the backseat and offered me a black baseball cap with a highway patrol logo.

"You didn't tell anyone you were bringing me, did you? Is that supposed to be a disguise?"

"It's not a disguise," he said. "It would be a crime to impersonate an officer of the law, and I would never ask you to do that. It's just a hat to keep the sun out of your eyes. Up to you if you want it."

I put it on and checked the mirror. No one was going to recognize me. No one would be thinking about Sarabeth Shepherd. Everyone would be focused on finding Destiny Jewell. That was the reason I'd come. For Destiny, and Abby.

"All good?" he said.

"Yeah."

"Just follow my lead. I'll handle most of the talking. All you have to do is look, listen, observe. Pay attention to your gut. You get a feeling about something, even if it doesn't seem important, let me know."

We got out and I trailed behind him as he approached the nearest man with a badge, the one who seemed to be in charge. I'd worried about being out of place, drawing attention, but there were plenty of other people milling around. A few were clearly law enforcement, but most were in plainclothes. Volunteers, maybe. Neighbors and friends who'd come to help. The community turning out to do what they could.

Farrow introduced himself to the deputy, who launched into an update of the situation, ignoring me. He gestured toward the house, where a woman stood in the shade, smoking a cigarette. The mother. She was rail thin, her long straw-colored hair parted in the middle and tucked tightly behind her ears. She wore torn jeans and a long-sleeved shirt despite the heat and could have passed as a teenager herself. Her hands were in constant motion, one fidgeting with the cigarette and flicking ash, the other pulling her hair behind her ears over and over. I worried that she'd mix up her hands, run the cigarette through her wispy hair, and light herself on fire. Farrow started toward her and I followed.

"Ms. Jewell?" Nick said. "I'm Nick Farrow, highway patrol."

"Trina," she said, blowing smoke out of the side of her mouth. Up close, she appeared weathered, like the Barbie doll Retta and I had accidentally left outside over the winter. Her skin was prematurely creased and splotched, her fingers knobbed with calluses, her hair fraying at the ends.

"Trina. I know you've already answered a lot of questions this morning, but I just want to go over a few things. Would that be all right?"

She nodded and kept nodding, her head cranking up and down as though she couldn't stop it once it got started.

"Want to sit down?" Farrow asked, gesturing to a pair of ratty lawn chairs.

"No-I'm-fine," she said. It all came out as one word.

"Okay. Can you tell me when you last saw Destiny?"

She flicked her cigarette with her thumb to knock off the ash, not noticing that it had burned down to the filter and gone out. "Wednesday night. The three of us ate supper together. Roasted hot dogs and let Destiny do some marshmallows." Trina shook her head, a sad smile crimping her lips together. "She liked 'em burnt, you know, let 'em catch fire and then blow 'em out. After that, she went out to the trailer to do her homework and Vance and me sat out here having a smoke till he had to leave for work. I guess it would've been about eight when I went in. I don't know exactly. It was dark, anyways, and the light was on in the trailer. That's the last I can be sure."

"Vance. He's your . . . ?"

"Boyfriend. Yessir."

"He live here with you?"

"Nah. Not, like, official. He lives with his mom in town, but he stays over here some when he's not working nights."

"Okay," Farrow said. "So you went inside. Did you hear anything in the night, get woken up at all?"

"No." Her head nicked to the side, like a horse shaking off flies. "Took an Ambien. Slept like the dead."

"What time does Destiny normally go to bed?"

She shrugged. "She stays up sometimes, reading, listening to music. I don't rightly know. Hard to tell with her out in the trailer."

We all turned to look at it. It was more of a camper than a

trailer, the kind you'd pull behind a truck on a family vacation, though it didn't look like it had been on any family vacations in a long time, if ever. It appeared to have settled into the red earth like a weary animal, never to heave up out of the dirt again.

"So she sleeps out there."

"Yeah. She was gettin' twitchy in the house, wanted her own bedroom. You know how teenagers are." She rolled her eyes. "Gotta have their *privacy.*" Trina pitched her cigarette butt toward a rusted coffee can sitting between the lawn chairs and missed, then pushed her hair back behind her ears with both hands.

"When did you notice Destiny was missing?"

"Woke up Thursday, had my coffee. I saw maybe around ten she hadn't let the chickens out yet, went and banged on the door and she didn't answer. Thought I'd better pull her outta bed, but she wasn't there. I was pissed, at first, figured she'd gone off without doing her chores." Trina tugged at her shirt collar. It was dark with sweat.

"Gone off? Where did you think she'd gone?"

"She likes to walk in the woods, spend the day outdoors, visit her friend across the holler. Loses track of time. Reckoned she'd be home in time for evening chores. When the sun went down, I lit a big fire in case she was trying to walk back in the dark. So she could find her way. I figured maybe she'd stayed too late at Hailey's house, decided to wait for daylight to head back. She's done that before."

"Did you try to call her, text her?"

"No, she don't have a phone anymore. Dropped it in the pond a while back and that was that. Told her she'd have to prove she's responsible if she wants a new one."

The sun pressed against my back, hot and insistent as an iron.

It still felt like summer here. Sweat greased the roots of Trina's pale hair and crept down to her forehead. She mopped her face with her shirtsleeve.

"When did you realize something was wrong?" Farrow asked.

"Friday morning when she still wasn't back, I got ahold of Hailey, but Destiny wasn't with her. So I got on Facebook, asked if anybody'd seen her. Nobody had, not since youth group Wednesday afternoon. Neighbors offered to come over and help look for her and one of 'em found her glasses in the trailer. It's her only pair, and she can't see worth shit without 'em, so she wouldn't take off and leave 'em behind."

Farrow nodded. "Do you know if she might have been communicating with someone online?"

"I don't know how she would. No internet out here. Sometimes she'd have to get online for school stuff. The homeschool group had a deal with the community center in town, the kids could go and use the Wi-Fi certain days." Trina squeezed her eyes shut and shook her head back and forth, back and forth. "I tried to raise her right, keep her safe. Protect her from all the horseshit out there."

"Mm-hm." Farrow paused for a moment while Trina took in a deep shuddering breath and wiped away tears. "You mentioned youth group. Which church?"

"Barren Branch," Trina croaked. "Just down the road a piece."

Music blared out of nowhere and I jumped, startled, knocking into Farrow's arm. Trina dug her phone out of her pocket and squinted at the screen while the chorus of "Don't Stop Believin'" played at top volume. "Gotta take this, sorry." We watched Trina disappear into the house, the phone pressed to her ear.

"You all right?" he said.

"Yeah," I said. "Fine."

"Let's check out the camper."

We crossed the yard, but I hung back as he stepped up on the cinder block that served as a step. "You sure it's okay for me to go in there?"

"It's already been processed, and it was compromised before that. Won't hurt for you to look."

We wedged ourselves into the doorway of the sweltering camper. Broken mini blinds hung askew in the windows. There was a narrow bunk against the wall and a shelf holding a few textbooks and a small collection of neatly folded shirts, underwear, and socks. A menagerie of well-worn stuffed animals lay on the floor, including a corduroy pig with button eyes and a grubby teddy bear that might have once been white. A Taylor Swift poster was tacked to the wall. It had been torn apart and taped back together. There was nothing on the bed, just a bare, dingy mattress, and I wondered if the bedding had been collected to check for evidence, if the stuffed toys had been tossed to the floor of the otherwise tidy room. The space had a musty, mothball odor and I felt the stagnant air pressing against my skin, seeping into my hair and clothing. I didn't want to breathe it in.

"Not much to see," I said, stepping down.

Farrow joined me, glancing at his phone. "I'd like to talk to the friend. Let me get some information from the sheriff and we can head out."

I walked back toward the truck, passing a group of elderly women who had set up a lunch station in the shade. "Hungry?" one of the ladies asked, extending a palsied arm to offer a sandwich on a paper plate. She wore a curly brown wig that had seen better days. "It's peanut butter with homemade jelly."

"Thank you," I said, accepting the wobbling plate before the sandwich could slide off.

"Have some water, too. It's awful hot out." She handed me a cup and I filled it from a cooler with a spigot. It was well water, I could tell, drawn up from dark veins in the earth, cold enough to crack your teeth. The woman eyed me as I wiped my mouth and refilled the cup.

"This kind of thing doesn't happen around here," she said.

I nodded, knowing she was wrong.

"Whereabouts you from?"

"Uh, St. Louis."

"Ah, you must be used to this kind of thing then, being from the city," she said. "Destiny was a country girl, through and through. A good girl. Hard worker. Loved Jesus. We share a table every week at the farmers market, her with her eggs and me with my plum jelly. But nobody'll be at the market today, I bet. Everybody's here, searching, praying. I'll pray for you, too, that you find her."

I took a bite of the sandwich as I walked away. The jelly was gritty and left an odd aftertaste. A group of men in Lone Ridge Volunteer Fire Department shirts gathered in a circle nearby, tightening their bootlaces and dousing themselves with bug spray, preparing to head out into the woods. I wondered if the man who took Destiny might be among the searchers, playing along, pretending to help. I closed my eyes behind my sunglasses, listened, like Farrow had said. There was the familiar Ozark twang, the distinctive dialect you didn't hear in the city—*cain't* instead of *can't*, *you'ns* instead of *you* or *y'all*. But no voice that I recognized.

"We're gonna spread out and make our way down to the base of the cliff," one of them said. "Check the ravine."

"Watch the trees, too. Me and my brother saw a deer go right over the edge of a bluff once, when we was hunting. Thought we'd find it down at the bottom, but it wasn't there. Couldn't figure how it got away. Days later we smelled it. It'd got stuck in a tree on the way down. It's probably still up there, skeleton hanging on a branch."

They were quiet for a moment. No one said Destiny's name, though they had to be imagining, as I was, her body broken on the rocks below or dangling from the trees. They gathered up their things and headed toward the woods. I breathed in deeply, checking for the scent of rot, but smelled only fresh air and cedar and a hint of smoke from the bonfire.

"Anything strike a chord?" Farrow asked, joining me.

"No."

"Well, let's get going," he said. "We're interviewing Destiny's friend."

As we made our way back to the main road, Farrow checked the odometer. "Driveway's more than two miles long. Kids do get snatched out in the country, but more often than not it's a crime of opportunity—the perp's driving around, comes across a kid riding a bike, or getting off a school bus in the middle of nowhere, all alone. How likely would it be that someone would drive all the way out here in the middle of the night, open up that camper, and randomly find a girl to take?"

"He knew she was there. He came for her."

"Yeah."

"So, what about me? I was alone, at the side of the road, in the middle of nowhere. Perfect opportunity for anybody driving by. That's how you said it usually happens, right?"

"Yes. But that doesn't mean it was random. Just that you were easier to find. If this was someone who knew Destiny, or knew where she lived, that's a pretty narrow group. She's fairly isolated.

Like you were. She's got her mom, church, homeschool, that's about it."

"One of the volunteers told me she sells eggs at the farmers market."

He shot me a look. "One more thing you have in common."

"But each girl went missing from a different place. We're spread out. If it's someone I know, someone from Wisteria, he'd stick out in some other small town."

"That's what we have to figure out," he said. "There's a connection. One of those common threads ties the three of you together and leads back to him. We just have to find it."

# CHAPTER 8

# SARABETH, THEN

## AGE 16

"So Eli's not coming?" Tom asked. He was trying hard to sound like he didn't care one way or the other, but he couldn't keep the disappointment from showing on his face. I felt a pinprick of guilt.

"He wanted to," I said. "He had to help Daddy with the tractor."

That wasn't quite a lie. Eli was helping Daddy, and he probably would have wanted to come, had he known about the invitation. He liked hanging out with Tom. But I looked forward to Secret Thursday all month, and I wasn't a hundred percent sure that I could trust Eli not to ruin it. He still seemed like his old self sometimes when our parents weren't around, but he'd started to take everything much more seriously, including our father's rules, and even though he'd accept the occasional illicit soda from the Darlings, I didn't think he'd approve of how far Tom and I had taken things. I couldn't risk losing the one small bit of freedom I had left.

Tom and I had perfected our routine, working together to get the baking done as quickly as possible and taking turns picking what we'd do the rest of the day. Today I'd chosen TV. Again.

"Do you want to maybe take the Gator out instead?" Tom asked. That was unusual, because even though TV was probably his last choice, he'd sometimes pick it for his own turn just because he knew I liked it best. He shook his head before I could respond. "Never mind. I'll get the snacks."

I covered the bread dough with a dishcloth and left it to rise. Tom grabbed a bag of Doritos, a box of Froot Loops, and two Cokes and carried them into the den. He closed the blinds to make it darker and then slid the pocket door shut before joining me on the couch. He seemed distracted, glancing at the door as he clicked through the channel guide.

"*Price Is Right* or *Little House on the Prairie?*" he said.

"Let's see which episode of *Little House.*"

"Oh, hey," Tom said. "'Sylvia.' Like your sister. That a good one?"

"Yeah," I said. "Let's watch it." I vaguely remembered that Sylvia was a girl Albert Ingalls had liked. Mainly I remembered that it was one of the few episodes where Albert got the main storyline. There weren't near enough of those. I was no longer ten years old and obsessed with the adventures of the Ingalls family, but my first crush wouldn't die.

Tom cracked open a Coke, and as he handed it to me I caught a whiff of cologne or aftershave, musk with a bitter edge of alcohol, like the old perfumes that had sat on my grandma's vanity for forty years and gone bad. I had never noticed Tom wearing aftershave before. I liked it, even if it was a little off. Perfume was something I associated with my old life, before my mother saw it as a sign of vanity and decadence. No one in my house ever smelled like anything but sweat or lye soap or woodsmoke.

We hadn't gotten very far into the episode before I realized it wasn't quite how I remembered it. Something very bad was happening to Sylvia. I glanced at Tom, who sat completely rigid, his hand submerged in the box of Froot Loops, his eyes locked on the screen. I had been younger when I'd watched it before, the darker tone lost on me amid my infatuation with Albert, the hints of abuse just confusing enough for ten-year-old me to know there was a bad guy without understanding exactly what he'd done. Now it made me think of Retta, how she'd told me something awful had happened, but I hadn't fully grasped what it was. I tried to push all of that away and focus instead on the romance between Sylvia and Albert. He loved her. He wanted to rescue her. Warmth flooded my body when their lips touched, when he kissed her in secret by the creek. I imagined him kissing me.

I felt a feathery sensation, Tom's fingers brushing against mine. His eyes widened, as though he'd startled himself by touching me. I leaned toward him before I could change my mind, inhaling the scent of his expired aftershave. He squeezed his eyes shut at the last second, like he was bracing for a crash, and I kissed him.

Tom tasted sweet, like the sugared cereal he'd been eating. I tried to pretend that it was Albert I was kissing, or Noah, or Jack, trying each one out to see how it felt, but even with my eyes closed, I couldn't forget that it was Tom. I pulled away and we wordlessly turned back to the TV, doing our best to pretend that nothing had happened.

"I better put in the first batch of cookies," I said.

"I can help."

"I've got it," I said. "Be right back. You can pick the next show. Or we can do something else."

I went down the hall to use the bathroom. After washing my

hands, I slid the vanity drawer open and carefully picked through Mrs. Darling's Avon lipstick samples, extracting a pale frosted pink. I drew a stripe on my palm, then looked in the mirror and dabbed the applicator to my lips. It was barely noticeable, but I liked the way it sparkled. I added a bit to my cheeks and rubbed it in, knowing I'd have to make sure every speck of glitter was wiped away before I went home.

When I opened the door, there was a half-naked man standing in the hall, blocking my way. He wore a thin flannel robe and boxer shorts, his hair disheveled, face unshaven, like he'd just woken up. The robe hung open, revealing a muscular chest, tattooed flames consuming his rib cage. I froze.

"Hey, pretty girl," the man said, his mouth stretching into a suggestive grin. "Who are you?"

"I . . . work for the Darlings," I said. The words came out before it could occur to me to ask who he was, what he was doing there in his underwear.

"Mm. So I guess that means you work for me?" He tucked one hand into the waistband of his boxers and let his gaze roll down my body and back up. I remembered the lipstick, the sparkles, and felt my face redden.

"What?"

"I'm part of the family," he said. "Probably the part they don't talk about. Ronnie Darling." He took his hand out of his pants and extended it.

I kept my arms at my sides. "I have to get back to work."

He stepped closer, his bare feet toeing the threshold. "What kind of work were you and Tommy doing in there with the door shut, hm? What would your daddy think?"

"Excuse me." I squeezed past him, scraping my arm on the doorframe to avoid touching him.

"Nice to meet you." He laughed but didn't follow me. I rushed down the hall and found Tom still in the den, the TV tuned to *Judge Judy*.

"There's a man," I said, not sure how to explain it.

The expression on Tom's face—horror and then shame—told me that he knew, and he was sorry. "He's some cousin of my grandpa's. He's just . . . visiting. I didn't think he'd come down. He sleeps all day."

"It just scared me for a second, I wasn't expecting to see anybody." My hands were still shaking.

"He's in the army. Grampa says he'll be going back soon. Did he say something to you?"

"Not much. He was . . . in a robe."

"We just try to ignore him," Tom said. "He mostly stays upstairs, in the spare room."

"Okay."

"He'll be gone soon," he said for the second time, as though saying it would make it true.

# CHAPTER 9

# SARAH, NOW

The Barneses' house was set deep in the woods, completely shrouded by oaks and cedars and snaking vines. There was no yard to speak of, no separation between the house and the forest. Scrub brush and saplings filled every space between the trees and crowded against the narrow front porch, reaching through the decaying spindles to scratch at our legs as we stood knocking on the storm door. Wasps drifted down from the eaves to drone about our heads. There was a chain wrapped around the porch post, and a dried-up water dish, but no dog in sight.

A face appeared behind the screen. Farrow held up his ID and introduced us. "I believe the sheriff called to let you know we were coming," he said. "We'd like to speak with Hailey Barnes."

The girl looked us over before replying. She had black chin-length hair that was swept dramatically to one side, covering half her face. "That's me," she said.

The door creaked open and she ushered us in. It was dark inside, and I imagined the house must be full of shadows at all times, with the trees closing in outside and a single jaundiced bulb dangling from the ceiling. On the coffee table, an old-fashioned oscillating fan rattled from side to side, its metal cage offering scant protection from the whirling blades.

"You can sit if you want," Hailey said, moving an overflowing laundry basket and a half-eaten bowl of cereal off the couch to make room. There was a long, sharp crack in the vinyl cushion, and I could feel it through my pants when I sat down, like a blade pressed to my skin.

Hailey straddled the arm of a recliner, careful not to disturb the fluffy white cat curled on the seat. She was dressed in a tank top, jean shorts, and army boots. She pushed her hair behind her ear, revealing a port-wine birthmark that stained the edge of her face from temple to jaw.

"Did you find her?" she said, looking stricken. "The sheriff wouldn't say, but I thought maybe, if they found her and she was . . ."

"No. No news yet. That's why we're here. Destiny's mother said she was close with the youth group at Barren Branch, and we think you all might be among the last people to see her before she disappeared. Did you notice anything out of the ordinary that day?"

Hailey picked at a ragged fingernail that had been chewed to the quick. "No. There was only three of us there, and Kenzie asked Pastor Brian for a one-on-one in the office, so me and Destiny just hung out and talked."

"Does the pastor often meet with you girls alone?"

Hailey caught the look on Farrow's face and rolled her eyes. "Oh, god, no. It's not like that. He's, like, the biggest prude. Saving his first kiss for his wedding day. Kenzie's just messing with him. She'll make up embarrassing stuff to talk about, like *sex* stuff, and ask him for spiritual guidance. He gets all nervous and sweaty. It's hilarious. More fun than listening to a sermon, you know?"

"Sure." Farrow nodded. The cat got up and stretched, then leapt to the floor to lick out the cereal bowl, the spoon clanging against the dish with each swipe of its tongue. "So, you and Destiny were alone. How did she seem? What did you talk about?"

"I don't know. She talked about Winter Meeting. She was wanting to get a new dress to wear, and I said maybe my sister could drive us to Jonesboro sometime so we could go shopping. I mean, it probably wasn't gonna happen, and it's not like we have any money to spend, but it was fun to think about, like, which places we'd go. Thrift stores. The mall. There's no place to shop around here."

"What's Winter Meeting?"

"It's a homeschool thing," she said. "Like, a big meeting for the home educators conference or whatever it's called. People come from all over the Ozarks. There's social stuff, too, some kind of dance, like a prom, I guess. If you're a homeschool kid, it's maybe the one time a year you get to do anything like that. It's a big deal. She always got excited about it."

Farrow shot me a quick glance. "Anything else?"

Hailey shook her head, her hair falling back over her eye and hiding the birthmark. "When Kenzie and Pastor Brian came out of the office, we did the closing prayer and left. Des texted me on her way home; that's the last I heard from her. I tried to get ahold of her when I found out she was missing, but never did."

"She texted you?" Farrow said the words slowly, and I could practically hear the gears whirring in his head.

"Yeah?" The cat rubbed against Hailey's legs, and she scooped it up into her lap.

"Could I see the text?"

"I deleted it. It wasn't anything important."

"You never know," Farrow said.

Hailey smirked, looking down at the threadbare carpet. "She asked if I thought Pastor Brian was trying to hide a boner when he came out of the office. He was walking kind of funny, holding the Bible over his crotch, but he wears those pants that are, like, pleated in front, so you can't really tell." Hailey stroked the cat, white hairs collecting on her black shirt and drifting into the air.

"Destiny's mother said she doesn't have a phone."

Hailey's hand froze midstroke. She glanced at me and then back to Farrow. "Her mom doesn't know. She hides it. It's one of those kind you get at the gas station."

"Oh," Farrow said. "Any particular reason she was hiding it?"

"I don't want to get her in trouble," Hailey said. "It's just that her mom's real strict about following rules, stuff like that. She'd take her phone away if she talked back or didn't do her chores or whatever. One time Trina caught her texting some guy and freaked out. There was nothing going on, it was just a kid from town, but she wasn't supposed to give her number to anybody without asking first. Trina told Des she'd have to crawl through the hog pen on her belly if she wanted her phone back. So she did it—got covered in mud and pig shit—and Trina told her to wash herself off in the pond. She got in the water and then Trina threw the phone in after her. Said she didn't want her daughter sneaking around talking to boys behind her back, and if she couldn't follow the rules with her phone, she couldn't have one."

"That sounds a bit over the top in terms of punishment. Was there any indication that Destiny was being abused at home?"

Hailey shrugged. "Trina never laid a hand on her that I know of. Most everybody around here's got strict parents. At school, if you get in trouble, they bend you over the principal's desk and swat you with a big wooden paddle just like in the old days. I mean, she used to complain about her mom sometimes, but Trina's kind of eased up since she started seeing Vance."

"Does Destiny get along all right with Vance?"

"Yeah, she likes him, I think. He convinced Trina to let her move out to the trailer. She was really happy, having her own space for the first time, her mom not being in her face 24/7. Seemed like things were pretty good."

"Destiny trusted you to keep her secret about the phone. Did she share any other secrets with you, good or bad? A relationship she might have wanted to keep hidden?"

"No." Hailey chewed her lip. "I was kind of jealous," she said. "About the trailer. I share a room with my sister. My dad sleeps on the couch with a shotgun by the door, and I always thought it was so we couldn't sneak out. I never worried anybody'd try to sneak *in*. You know?"

Farrow nodded solemnly and handed Hailey a business card. "One of the sheriff's detectives will follow up with you. In the meantime, if you think of anything else, give me a call on my cell."

We got back on the road, the sun blinding after the enveloping darkness at the Barnes house. "The Winter Meeting she was talking about," Farrow said. "Are you familiar with that?"

"Yeah. We went every year when I was in high school. My mother was on a committee. She took me and my sister."

"I wonder if Abby went," he said. "I'll have to check."

"You think it could be somebody from the conference?"

"It's a possible connection. It could be a coincidence that you were all homeschooled, but if you all attended this same event, were exposed to the same people—that might narrow it a bit. It's worth looking into."

"What about the phone? Can you trace it or something?"

"Maybe. They could try to get call records, see if that turns up any suspects. That'll take time. Hailey said Destiny kept the phone hidden, so if she was taken in the night, without her glasses, I'm wondering if the phone's still there, stowed away someplace her mother wouldn't know to look."

"So what now?"

"Need to find a gas station, for starters, if we don't want to get stuck out here. I'm hoping there's one up ahead, by the river, so we don't have to drive all the way back to town."

As the road curled down into the river valley, a deep, forested ravine opened up on the passenger side, the white line crumbling into the chasm, no guardrail, no room for error. I wanted to shut my eyes but didn't dare. I dug my fingernails into the upholstery and focused on Farrow's hands, willing them to stay steady on the wheel, as though my vigilance alone might keep us from plunging over the edge. Just before the bridge, the valley flattened out and a gas station appeared, a rustic log cabin with two pumps out front and a sign that said CASH ONLY. The windows were papered over with beer and cigarette ads.

Farrow pumped gas, phone to his ear. I got out to throw away our coffee cups and wandered to the edge of the lot to look down at the river. A steep stone path led through the weeds to a row of tiny tin-roofed cabins perched at the water's edge beneath a canopy of cottonwoods. Sparrows trilled in the tall grass. The river frothed over shallow rapids and glittered green where the sun struck. Despite the undeniable beauty of the landscape, tension threaded through my body, urging my heart to pump faster, the hills and hollers forever linked to my old life and the thirst to escape it. I wondered if Destiny had been content here, or if she felt that same longing to get out.

Farrow went inside to pay. When he came back, he had a paper bag and two candy bars, and he offered one to me.

"There's a prayer vigil tonight at the Jewells' farm, starting at dusk," he said. "There'll be a bonfire. All are welcome."

"You think we should go," I said. "And you're trying to bribe me with a Mr. Goodbar?"

"Sorry," he said. "Slim pickings in there." His brow furrowed. "I promised I'd get you home tonight, and I will, if that's what you want. But I think we need a little more time here. Need to see who shows up at the vigil, how they act. See if we can find that phone. What do you think?"

"I think you never had any intention of going back tonight. I think you only said that to get me here."

He didn't deny it. "It's up to you," he said. "I'm not going to force you into anything."

"Anything else, you mean." As much as I wanted to be done with this, he was right, we weren't done. Abby and Destiny still weren't home. I had already come all this way, and I would do everything I could. I sighed and took the candy bar.

"Is that a yes?"

"You could have at least told me to bring a toothbrush."

He shook the paper bag. "I've got you covered. And I went ahead and booked two cabins, just in case. The clerk said not to worry, they scrubbed them out 'real good' after the flood."

"Great."

We got back in the Tahoe and I texted Helen to ask how Gypsy was doing. She sent a pic of the dog sprawled on a leather sofa, belly up, sound asleep. I wished that I could trade places with her, that I could sleep on Helen's couch instead of in a rickety cabin on a riverbank, not far from where Destiny had gone missing.

*I might be late,* I typed. *Can you keep her until tomorrow?*
*Of course! Everything okay?*

I sent a thumbs-up. It felt like less of a lie than saying every-thing was fine.


Nearly two dozen vehicles snaked up the dirt road and parked in the Jewells' field as dusk crept in. Farrow and I had spent the af-ternoon assisting the deputies in a fruitless search for Destiny's phone. The bonfire snapped and roared, devouring stacks of dry brush and sending sparks into the cool evening air. Trina stood in the firelight with her boyfriend, Vance, at her side and greeted each person in turn, like a receiving line at a wedding or a fu-neral, while a plainclothes detective looked on. The detective was not exactly undercover—everyone from town knew who he was and called him by name. Farrow and I stayed in the shadows, watching and listening. Most of the people in attendance seemed to be friends of the Jewells or to know them from church, though there were several with no apparent connection: a man from the Rotary club, prayer leaders from neighboring churches, a mother grieving the loss of her own teenage daughter, who'd drowned in the river on the Fourth of July. She had heard about the vigil on Facebook. I studied the group from Barren Branch and guessed which one was Pastor Brian: a slight twenty-something in pleated khakis, a Bible jammed in his armpit. He wore a stunned expres-sion and a helmet of yellow Ken-doll hair.

Trina wiped manically at her tears as Pastor Brian spoke to her, and Vance wrapped his arm around her shoulders, holding her close. Vance and Trina could have been brother and sister. They had the same pale, scraggly hair, lanky build, and weath-ered skin. He counterbalanced Trina's fidgeting with slow, deliberate motions, holding Brian's hand rather than pumping it, standing steady while Trina's head bobbed up and down, up and down.

When darkness had fully set in and the group gathered together to clasp hands and pray, Farrow motioned for me to join him and we slipped away from the fire, to the far side of Destiny's trailer.

"It would've been dark like this when he took her," Farrow said. "The only light's coming from the porch at the front of the house. If he wanted to stay out of sight, he would've come this way, from behind the trailer. He could've kept his cover all the way from the road and back." He aimed his flashlight into the brush, swept the beam back and forth. "If she dropped her phone or anything else, it might be somewhere along here."

"We already looked back here. We looked everywhere."

"Yeah, but it'd be easy to overlook something in all this brush. I thought maybe a phone would catch the light. Reflect, you know, like cats' eyes."

We walked in the direction of the road, watching the weeds as the light moved over them, waiting for something shiny to wink at us from the dark. Over in the field, the group began to sing. *Why should I feel discouraged? And why should the shadows come?* "His Eye Is on the Sparrow." It was a hymn I knew well, one my mother had often sung as a lullaby.

Farrow stopped, turned around, walked in a circle. Beyond the trailer and the house, the fire whistled and cracked, orange flames streaming upward into the night as the people sang. *His eye is on the little sparrow . . . He's watching over you and me.*

"Do you feel that?" Farrow said.

"What?"

"The ground. Most of it around here, it's rock and clay. But it feels a bit softer here. I didn't notice anything different in day-light, but now, you can tell it's loose underfoot. Tilled up, maybe. Could be a garden spot. Or something else."

I turned my back to the fire and the farm. The night sky was stunning, black and clear, the stars bright and piercing. I'd learned nothing about astronomy in homeschool and had only recently discovered, from watching the Discovery Channel, that a number of the stars we saw were long dead, their light just now reaching us from distant space.

"How do you know," I said, "in situations like this, when the families are isolated, the kids don't go to school . . . where it's normal for no one outside the family to see them for days on end . . . how can you really know what happened?"

Farrow nodded. "It complicates things," he said. "But we check the timeline we have, we talk to the family and people who know them. We look at the evidence. And we cover our bases."

"How?"

"Cadaver dogs are coming in the morning," he said. "Just in case."

# CHAPTER 10

# SARABETH, THEN

## AGE 17

Cousin Ronnie had not gone back to the army. Apparently, an unfortunate misunderstanding had caused his early discharge from the armed services. He had failed to mention that when he showed up at the Darlings' house, but when it became clear that he wasn't leaving, he confessed that he had nowhere else to go. Mr. and Mrs. Darling were trying to help him get back on track, as they put it. Mr. Darling said three things were guaranteed to help a struggling soul: God, family, and honest work. Mrs. Darling added home cooking to the list. For months they'd been feeding him, taking him to church, and paying him to help out on the farm. He had been a mechanic in the army and was teaching Tom, and sometimes Eli, how to work on the tractors and other bits of machinery. Mr. and Mrs. Darling had convinced themselves that he was truly making progress and bettering himself, because they badly wanted to believe that he would one day move out of their house.

It was supposed to be Secret Thursday, but Ronnie had planted himself at the kitchen table while I baked, pretending to read the Bible. He wore tight jeans and a camouflage T-shirt with the sleeves cut off so his biceps were on display.

"You must know the Bible pretty well," he said.

I shrugged, my hands buried in dough. I had to bake more bread since Ronnie had come to stay. He would eat half a pan of rolls before they even had time to cool, shoving them down his throat one after another, like a snake swallowing eggs in the hen-house.

"You know Song of Songs? I'm having trouble following. Maybe you can explain it to me." He got up from the table and leaned against the counter next to me, holding the Bible up so he could read aloud. "'Your two breasts are like two fawns, twins of a gazelle, that graze among the lilies.' I mean, it's kinda dirty, right? What exactly is it supposed to teach me?"

I kept kneading the dough, hoping if I ignored him he would get bored and leave me alone. He set the Bible down and angled closer to me, his face inches from mine. His breath warmed my cheek, but I didn't want to give him the satisfaction of shrinking away.

"What's the matter, are you scared to talk to me? Look, I know you're not some holy roller. You're stuck here pretending to be something you're not, just like me. What are you, sixteen, seventeen? Wearing a fucking apron, baking bread all day? Don't tell me you don't want to take off that ugly old-lady dress and get out of here for a while, have some fun. I could help you out with that. You ever want to go for a ride, just say the word."

Tom, who'd been in his room all morning, walked in and saw us standing there, my face burning. "Oh," he said. "I was gonna see if you needed help."

I wiped sweat off my forehead with my sleeve. "That's okay,"

I said. "I'm almost done." Tom glared at Ronnie and stalked out of the kitchen. We heard a door slam.

"Now that is somebody who does not know how to have a good time," Ronnie said, smirking. "You know, I used to figure him for queer, but it almost seems like he gets jealous when I talk to you. Like he thinks there's something going on between us. Wonder why that is."

I threw the dough in the bowl and he chuckled, brushing against me on his way out the door. Through the window, I watched him strut toward the barn. He stood in the sunshine and stripped off his shirt, revealing a massive black scorpion tattooed down his spine. He was ruining everything. The Darlings' house had felt different ever since he arrived. Tom was irritable and barely left his room. Mr. and Mrs. Darling were distracted, focusing all their energy and attention on Ronnie. Still, my job provided a measure of freedom, a respite from home, and I didn't want to lose that. If I told my parents about Ronnie's behavior, they wouldn't let me go to the Darlings' anymore. Mama would probably ask what I'd done to encourage him, if I'd given him the wrong kind of smile.

Ronnie seemed to have figured out that I wasn't going to tell on him, that he could say anything he pleased and I would stand there and take it. From what I'd seen so far, though, he was mostly talk, and if I could tune out Pastor Rick's sermons and my mother's constant lecturing, I could surely manage to ignore him. I told myself he wouldn't go so far as to lay a hand on me, though I remembered Tom saying Ronnie would be gone soon, repeating it over and over to convince himself, but that hadn't made it true. There was no telling what Ronnie might do.

# CHAPTER 11

# SARAH, NOW

It was late when we left the Jewells' farm and headed back to our cabins for the night. There were no other cars on the road. As we began our descent into the river valley, the headlights reflected a dark stain, the blacktop gleaming with fresh blood. It must have been a deer, or something of similar size. There was no sign of a body. Maybe the animal had managed to hobble away, or someone had taken it to salvage the meat.

The gas station was closed when we arrived, all the lights out. We drove down the hill and parked on the rocky shore. Farrow reached into the paper bag and handed me a toothbrush and a key attached to a chunk of antler. He watched as I stepped onto my cabin's tiny porch and unlocked the door, making sure I got safely inside. I flicked the light on and waved good night before locking the door behind me.

I kept my hand on the knob as I surveyed the low-ceilinged room, which contained nothing but a bed and a nightstand, no unnecessary comforts or frills. It smelled of mildew and decay, the lingering dampness of a flood. The walls, floor, and ceiling were all a mottled brown, perfect for hiding insects and stains. The overhead light didn't quite reach into the corners. I took out my phone to shine the flashlight behind the bed. The space glittered with an impressive network of spiderwebs. The bedding was the color of dried blood, dusty to the touch, and I wondered when it had last been washed, how long it had been since someone stayed here in the off-season.

There were three windows, one by the front door, one above the bed, and one directly across from it. Each had a makeshift curtain that was too short to reach the sill, leaving a gap for someone to see in, though I told myself there was no one outside for miles, no one but Farrow. All the other cabins were empty.

I stepped into the tiny bathroom and slung back the shower curtain, revealing a large, leggy spider near the drain. I leaned down and got close enough to make out the telltale fiddle on its head: a brown recluse. Our house on the farm with its gaps and drafts had harbored all manner of spiders and crawling things, including scorpions and the occasional snake, but recluses made me especially nervous. My brother Luke had been bitten in bed, the venom inducing fever and infection, rotting a hole the size of a silver dollar in his leg. I climbed into the tub to smash the spider, but when I lifted my foot, it jumped onto my shoe. I kicked and screamed until it disappeared into the folds of the shower curtain. Moments later, Farrow was pounding at my door and I hurried to open it.

"You okay? Thought I heard something."

"Yeah," I said, still breathless. "It was just . . . a spider. How did you even hear me?"

"Uh, you were pretty loud. And I was sitting right outside. Didn't feel like going in quite yet." He gestured toward a pair of

Adirondack chairs overlooking the river. "I've got some warm Gatorade if you'd like to join me."

"Sure," I said, grateful for an excuse to get out of the cabin. "No Gatorade. But I'll hang out for a minute." I pulled the door shut behind me and Farrow and I sat side by side in the darkness, listening to the water flow over the rocks. Across the river, the woods formed a black abyss beneath the stars.

I liked being outside at night. Sometimes at home I'd sit on the porch when I couldn't sleep. It was true that certain kinds of darkness made me uneasy. I didn't like the way a windowless room or a blindfold closed in on you. But there was a difference between the dark of confinement and the dark of night. The night sky felt open, expansive, full of promise. It was never completely void of light, though it might come awfully close in a place like this.

"I hope she's okay," I said.

"Me too." He leaned back in the chair, looking up at the sky. "I wish we'd made more progress today. The window's so small, and the longer someone's missing . . ."

"We got here as quick as we could."

"No. We came as soon as we heard. But we were already behind. She's been gone since Wednesday night." He picked at the splintered wood on the armrest and then turned toward me, his face ashen in the moonlight. "Your parents never contacted the police. Something I was thinking about . . . your father said they assumed you'd taken off on your own, and they saw no reason to get the law involved. They preferred to keep private matters private. Why did they think you'd left?"

The chill in the air grew sharper as a breeze swept through the river valley, and a light fog drifted up from the water. "It was no secret I wanted to get out of there. I wanted to go to college and they wanted to force me to marry a man I barely knew. They didn't like me pushing back. I got into some trouble, right before. Said some things. I guess it made sense to them that I'd leave."

"Have you talked to them about it, now that some time has passed?"

"No," I said. "I don't hear from them much. They don't have a phone, or email. My mother and I exchange letters sometimes, but we don't talk about any of that."

"Do you miss them?"

A moth flitted along my bare arm, and I brushed it away. "I'm not sure how that's relevant to the case."

"It's not," he said, his voice soft. "I just wondered."

"Yeah. I miss my little sister. Sylvie. We were really close, and I feel like I abandoned her. I worry sometimes that she's forgotten me, or my mother's turned her against me. I got a letter—" I stopped myself. I hadn't told anyone, hadn't had anyone to tell.

Farrow nudged gently. "And?"

"My mother said Sylvie's getting married. I don't know if it's something she wants, or if they're forcing it on her, like they tried to with me. I feel like it's all my fault, that it wouldn't have happened if I'd been there looking out for her, protecting her."

"You can't blame yourself for leaving," he said. "And it might not have been any different if you were still there. But I get it. I have a little sister. Or I did. Half sister."

"Had? What happened to her?"

"Our family split up when we were kids. Lost touch."

"Oh. Bad divorce?"

"No."

I waited for him to continue, but he didn't. "No? That's it? You've been quizzing me about my family all day, and I've told you everything. You can't tell me one thing about yours?"

"Okay," he said. "You're right. That's fair. We lost touch because we got taken away and put in foster care. Neither of our dads was around. Our mom worked nights at a convenience store and paid a woman in our building to sleep over while she was gone. One night the sitter didn't show, and we were fine, so then Mom figured we didn't need anybody watching us. We were just sleeping, anyway. Save a few bucks, and we didn't have any to spare. Someone reported her and family services got involved. Mom couldn't keep it together after that. She wanted to get us back, but she lost her job, got evicted, moved in with her boyfriend, who was running a meth house. She wound up in prison. DFS didn't want to separate us, but in the end, my sister and I got adopted by different families."

"I'm sorry," I said. "So you haven't seen her since then?"

"No. Her adoptive family moved around a lot. We used to do birthday cards, phone calls, but that stopped after a while. I wanted to reconnect, apologize. When I tracked down her parents, they weren't open to a reunion. She's still a minor, so there wasn't much I could do."

"What did you want to apologize for?"

"I was the reason our family split up," he said. "I was talking to a kid at school, bragging, how I had the place to myself at night. Like I was partying or something while my mom was at work. A teacher heard me, asked some questions. I was twelve years old, scared of every noise, worried my baby sister'd wake up and start crying and I wouldn't know what to do. Teachers are mandatory reporters. So."

"You were a kid. It wasn't your fault. Sounds like it was a bad situation to begin with."

"I know. But I wonder how things might've turned out if I

could have just held it together. She never did wake up crying. Not once."

"Well, you can tell her all that when you see her. I bet she won't hold it against you. Maybe her new life is really great."

"Yeah." Farrow stretched his shoulders, ticked his head side to side to crack his neck. "I'm gonna get to bed. The dogs'll be at the farm first thing in the morning." He pulled himself out of the chair. "You staying up for a bit, or . . . ?"

"I don't think I can sleep in there," I said.

"Oh. We can switch cabins if you want. Or I can come kill the spider."

"I'm not scared of spiders." I didn't know how to explain that it wasn't the cabin, or the bugs, or anything he could fix. It was this place, so much like home, that made me uneasy—the isolation, the yawning emptiness waiting to swallow me up. I wanted to go back to St. Agnes, to my little house tucked in among all the other houses, the city lighting up the horizon.

He was silent for a moment, and I could feel him watching me. He dug his keys out of his pocket and handed them over. "You can sleep in the truck if you'd like. Lock yourself in. I've done it before. It's not that comfortable, but there's room to stretch out in the back."

"Thanks."

"Call if you need me," he said. "Or hit the horn. I'm a light sleeper, and I'll only be ten feet away."

I found a jacket of Farrow's to use as a pillow and lay across the bench seat, watching the stars, listening to the urgent whisper of the river. The jacket smelled like him, the faint scent of fresh-cut grass lingering from his soap or cologne. I performed my nighttime rituals, checking and rechecking the windows and locks, counting slow, deep breaths, reminding myself that I was safe, for the moment at least. The light in Farrow's cabin was still burning as I drifted toward sleep, though he hadn't gone inside. I could just make out his dark silhouette on the shore, keeping watch.

# CHAPTER 12

# SARABETH, THEN

## AGE 17

Ronnie had ruined Secret Thursdays, but I had found something new to look forward to at the Darlings' house. I'd finished my homeschooling, and my parents wouldn't let me enroll in community college since they'd decided I should get married instead, but I'd convinced Mama to allow me to take an online class. The compromise was that she got to choose the course. She claimed it was an introduction to nursing, one of the few careers she deemed acceptable for me, but it was offered through an educational group I'd never heard of, not a real school, and by the second class, I realized it was a thinly veiled attempt to train women in unlicensed midwifery. I didn't care. I had no interest in nursing, no desire to usher babies into the world with the accompanying blood and screams. All I cared about was the time it gave me away from home.

Tom had agreed to let me use his laptop, and Mrs. Darling had cleared off a tiny desk in her sewing room for me. She tucked a bouquet of sweet peas in an old perfume bottle and placed it on the windowsill where it would catch the light. The room smelled like fabric softener, the name-brand kind my grandma used to get, with the teddy bear on the box. I could sit down and shut the door and everyone would leave me alone for one blessed hour. I could feel my shoulders loosening on the walk to their house.

On the day of my first exam, which I hadn't bothered to study for, Tom met me at the door before I could knock, his face flushed. "You can't use my computer today," he said.

"Why not?"

He looked over his shoulder, into the house, and then turned back to me. "Gramma took it away," he whispered. "I think she found . . . porn on it, or something, and I know it was Ronnie, but she probably thinks it was me."

My stomach knotted. I knew I should feel bad for Tom, but I was more worried for myself, that Mrs. Darling might have found out I'd been messing around on the internet and would tell my parents. "Are you sure it was porn?" I said.

"No, but definitely something bad. What else could it be?"

"She has to know it was him," I said. "Maybe she just took it for evidence, and she's going to confront him with it and make him leave."

"I wish," he said. "I know you were supposed to do your class stuff, but since you can't, I think you should probably leave."

"If I go back home now, my mother'll ask what's going on."

"I don't know, tell her we're sick or something. Or the internet's down."

"Tommy!" Mrs. Darling called out from somewhere inside the house.

"Sorry," he said, leaving me alone on the porch as the door swung shut.

I walked up the road to the farm stand, not knowing where else to go. I didn't want to go home. I wanted to sneak up to the

Darlings' window and eavesdrop, find out what was happening. My mother had made a big deal about trusting me online, and I'd tried to be careful, knowing she had likely enlisted Mrs. Darling to keep an eye on me. Tom had shown me how to erase the browser history. I'd turn on the class lecture and let it play while I shopped for earrings and jeans and makeup that I couldn't buy or wear, logged in to Tom's Instagram to look up my old school friends, and googled things my parents wouldn't want me to google. The last time I'd been on the computer, I'd started out searching for the nearest bus station and ended up on a site for women who'd escaped arranged marriages. Many of them had been raised in polygamist sects. To get out, they'd had to take risks, trust strangers, leave everything behind, start their lives over with nothing.

I'd been so absorbed in their stories that I kept reading long after my class finished and was startled when Mrs. Darling knocked on the door to check on me. Now I couldn't remember whether I'd gone back and deleted my history. Mrs. Darling was always kind and generous toward me, but she wouldn't want to betray my parents' trust. If she saw what I'd been looking at, there was a good chance that she would call and tell them. Maybe she already had. Acid burned my throat. Mama might never let me out of the house again.

I was too preoccupied to notice that a vehicle had pulled up until I heard a door shut. It was Jack. I waited for his friends to pile out of the Jeep, but he was alone. He'd never come alone before.

"Hey," he said, sheepish. He pushed his sun-streaked hair out of his face and then stuffed his hands into the pockets of his cargo shorts. He somehow managed to look like a surfer despite being landlocked in the Bible Belt.

"Hi."

"Here by yourself?"

"Yeah," I said. "We're not really open today. I was out for a walk."

"Oh," he said. "I didn't come to buy anything."

"I know," I said. "You never do."

"Right." He smiled, closemouthed. He'd smiled like that since his front teeth came in crooked in grade school, and the habit stuck even though he'd had braces since then. "I just wanted to apologize," he said. "For the other day. My friends are jerks sometimes." I assumed he was referring to the bare ass hanging out the window of his Jeep when he drove by the week before, one of them mooning me, though I wondered why he was apologizing now, out of all the times his friends had made crude jokes and gestures and he hadn't said a word.

"It's fine," I said. "I'm used to it."

He tilted his head. "If you're not working . . . wanna go for a ride?"

Heat spread across my chest. I had imagined something like this, played out a dozen different ways—Jack and I cruising downtown on a Saturday night, or going for ice cream at the Dairy Queen, or playing basketball in his driveway like we did when we were kids—though I'd given up hope that it would ever happen. My parents wouldn't allow me to go for a ride with a boy from town, even if it was Jack, who had once been my closest friend. I knew I should say no, but I didn't care anymore. What could they do that would make my life worse than it already was? They were planning to marry me off, and if they found out I was searching for ways to escape, they might lock me in the house until the wedding. I might as well take a ride with Jack while I had the chance.

"Sure," I said. "I've got an hour or so before I have to get home."

"Oh." He faltered for a moment, caught off guard, but quickly recovered, his mouth again stretching into a tight-lipped smile. "All right. Let's go."

We sped away from Wisteria, going too fast, riding the center line on the curves. Jack tapped on his phone, one hand on the wheel as he texted, the wind from the open windows whipping our hair. He hadn't looked at me once since we started to drive, hadn't spoken a word. I tried to enjoy the fleeting rush of freedom, to forget what might await me at home, but the harder I tried to relax, the tenser I grew. We were miles from town when he cut off the main road, the Jeep bouncing over deep ruts, following a faint path through the woods and finally stopping in a glen filled with cottonwood trees. I'd thought, somehow, that we'd keep driving in silence, away from town and then back. It hadn't occurred to me that we would stop.

"It's so pretty," I said, the words coming out stilted. "Where are we?"

"It's my granddad's land. There's a creek, a swimming hole just upstream. It's spring fed, though, turn you blue right quick."

I imagined the two of us wading into the frigid water, the breathless shock of biting cold on warm skin, Jack shirtless in the sun. My last summer in town, Jack's parents had set up a flimsy aboveground pool and invited all the families on our block over for a Fourth of July party. Daddy had stood around the grill, laughing and drinking beer with all the other dads, paying no attention as I played with my friends. Jack and I had floated in the pool while darkness fell around us, and in the moment of anticipation before the fireworks began to crack overhead, he had kissed me on the cheek. I'd always wondered if he meant to kiss me on the lips instead, if he'd miscalculated or lost his courage.

"You still have that pool in your backyard?"

He let out a short laugh and then turned to look at me, a warm flash of recognition in his eyes, as though the shared memory had proven that I was really me, not an impostor in a prairie dress. "Nah," he said. "It got busted by the end of the summer. I'd pretty much forgot about it. Fun while it lasted, though."

"I don't think I've been swimming since then."

"Really? Why not?"

"My mom threw away my swimsuit. She threw out most of my stuff when we moved. Or took it to Salvation Army." Bitterness welled up at the thought of it. When I found her emptying my closet, I'd tried to tear my things away from her. I screamed that I hated her, and she slapped me so hard I spun around and fell to my knees.

Jack shifted in his seat, rested his hand on the console between us. "When you left," he said, "it was weird. There were all these garbage bags piled on your driveway, furniture, your TV. I went and looked in the windows and the house was empty. Nobody knew what happened—you just disappeared. Kids at school said your family joined a cult. The first time I drove out this way and saw you by the road—how long had it been, two years? I wanted to talk to you, really talk to you, but I didn't know what to say. You looked different. And the guys . . ."

"I know. It's okay."

He checked the time on the dashboard and glanced in the rearview mirror. There was nothing to see but trees, dense woods on all sides.

"I know it's been a while," I said. "But I still think of us as friends. I like to see you, even if we don't get to talk or hang out like we used to. It makes me feel almost . . . normal. Or at least, makes me remember what normal feels like."

"So what's the deal with your family, anyway? Do you live on a commune or something?"

"No. It's just a regular farm."

"Your clothes . . . your hair?" He reached out and I imagined him stroking my hair where it hung loose over my shoulder, his fingertips gliding down my arm, but he barely brushed my sleeve before he drew back.

I looked down at my dress, shapeless, utilitarian, ugly. "The church we're at now, it's . . . old-fashioned. And really strict. Women are supposed to act a certain way, dress a certain way, basically do what they're told."

"Wow," he said. "Sounds kinda creepy."

"Yeah," I said. "It is. I just have to go along with it till I can leave."

Jack chewed his lip. His appearance had changed subtly since middle school, the boyish softness now gone from his face, but his mannerisms were the same.

"Can I ask you something?" I said.

"Sure."

"Could you help me get out? I was thinking of taking a bus. But I don't have any money or any way to get to the station."

He squinted, confused. "You . . . want me to take you to a bus station and buy you a ticket? Where would you go?"

"I don't know. Anywhere. I don't have anyone else to ask."

The rumble of an approaching engine reached the clearing, and Jack nervously checked the mirror again. "Is somebody coming?" I asked.

He rubbed his palm over his face. "Shit," he said. "It was stupid. A dare."

"What are you talking about?"

"My friends. Everett. They wanted me to bring you out here, and . . ."

"And what?"

He shook his head. "I'm sorry. I didn't think you'd come."

They were getting closer. I heard brush snapping under tires, country music blaring. Anger flared inside me, burning away any fear. I'd been stupid to think that he cared about me after all this time, that someone who wouldn't even speak to me would suddenly decide to invite me for a ride.

"*Jack.*"

He threw the Jeep in gear and peeled out, kicking up dead leaves. We swerved around the truck that barreled toward us, Everett laying on the horn. Something smashed into the back of the Jeep and I flinched. Behind us, in the mirror, a punctured beer can danced over the rocks, spraying foam into the air. Jack's phone kept buzzing as we drove away, but he didn't answer it. "I wouldn't have let anybody hurt you," he said. "It was supposed to be a joke."

I didn't say anything, didn't look at him when he said, *Sarabeth, please,* or when he let me out at the side of the road and drove off. I started down my driveway and spied Tom across the field, heading toward his house. I hollered his name, but he kept walking, so I chased after him.

"Hey," I said when I caught up.

"Hey. I was looking for you." He pushed his shirtsleeves up, but they immediately slid back down his skinny arms. "You okay? Your face is all red."

"Yeah, I was just . . . running. What did your grandma say?"

"She's taking the computer in to get some kind of internet

controls installed so she can track every single thing anybody does."

"Did she call my mother?"

He shrugged. "She didn't say anything about you. I didn't want to ask."

I'd find out soon enough, when I got home.

"I saw you get out of that Jeep," he said. "Was that Jack?"

"Yeah."

"Where did you go?"

"Nowhere." He knew I was lying, and his face pinched up like I'd betrayed him somehow, but I didn't want to tell him what had happened. He took a couple of steps back and turned around without a word, walking away, leaving me alone on the hill.

# CHAPTER 13

# SARAH, NOW

There was a police cruiser parked in the yard when we arrived at the Jewells'. The sheriff stood beneath a tree, scrolling on his phone and frowning, and Farrow went to join him. I crossed the yard, dew dampening my shoes. A fresh pile of brush had been stacked in the firepit, low flames just beginning to lick up through the branches. Trina stood at the edge of the still-smoldering ashes, squinting at the rising sun, sucking on a cigarette. She wore the same rumpled clothing she'd had on the night before, just like me, and I wondered if she'd gotten any sleep.

"Hey," Trina said, nodding. She threw her spent cigarette into the fire and cracked her knuckles, one after another, working left to right and then back again. A dry laugh choked out of her throat. "I got up thinking she'd overslept, that she forgot to let the chickens out again. I was fixing to pull her outta bed."

"I'm so sorry," I said. I wasn't sure what else to say.

She twisted her hands like she was wringing out a dishrag. A truck rumbled up the drive, but Trina didn't bother to turn around and look. The sheriff walked over and she didn't look at him either.

"Dogs are here," he said.

"They didn't find nothing yesterday," Trina said.

He cleared his throat. "These are special dogs. Cadaver dogs."

"Cadaver?" Trina turned to face him.

"They can detect . . . remains."

She stood perfectly still for a moment as the word sank in, and then her face crumpled in anguish. "You're saying . . . you think she's *dead*? You think my daughter is *fucking dead*?" She doubled over, and the howl that ripped out of her mouth reminded me of a tornado siren, a warning to take cover. The sheriff reached out to her and she yelped and spun away, stumbling into me and unexpectedly grasping me in a fierce embrace, her arms stiff as wire hangers. She reeked of smoke and sweat. I let her sob in my ear until her grip loosened and then helped her to one of the lawn chairs so she could sit down.

"Will you stay with me?" she said, her voice raw.

"Of course."

She took out a cigarette but didn't light it. I sat in the chair next to her and we watched as the two dogs and their handlers moved around the yard and through the field to the edge of the woods. They went in and out of the trailer, the main house, the barn and sheds, circled Trina's truck.

Farrow watched, too, from the other side of the yard, his phone to his ear much of the time. When the dogs finished up, he and the sheriff conferred with the handlers and then finally came to give us the news.

The sheriff shook his head. Trina sucked in a long breath and blew it out through pursed lips.

"Nothing?" she said.

"No. We'll wrap up here and head out. We've got some leads to follow up on, and we'll keep you posted. Hopefully we'll have some news real soon."

Trina got up, lit her cigarette, and went in the house. Farrow and the sheriff huddled for a minute, their voices low, and then they shook hands and the sheriff walked away.

"What about that spot behind the trailer?" I asked. "The loose soil?"

"They worked the dogs over that area pretty thoroughly, and they didn't mark anything. Looks like a garden patch, most likely, not a fresh dig. Couldn't push a stick more than a few inches down. Not deep enough to bury a body."

"So what now?"

"If she's not here, she's out there somewhere. Sheriff's department's going to conduct more interviews, talk to people. Put out a plea for security footage, deer cameras, doorbell videos, anything from around the time she disappeared. I've got some individuals to follow up on from the sex offender registry. But first, I'm going to get you home like I promised. I'd like to make a stop on the way back, though, if it's okay with you. It's a bit of a detour."

"Where?"

"Highway 65. Just south of Branson."

He really was desperate. It wouldn't help, but I had promised him that I would do everything I could, and I knew he wouldn't give up until he had crossed off every last thing.


"Almost there," Farrow said. "Try closing your eyes. Maybe that'll spark something."

I tried, but all it did was make me carsick. I couldn't tell if the hills and curves felt familiar, couldn't remember how long we had traveled on the smooth four-lane road as opposed to the two-lane blacktop. I didn't know if we were on the same route that my abductor had taken that night. I could barely remember anything from that ride, because at the time, I'd been terrified that I was about to die.

"This is it," he said.

We exited the highway and pulled into the roadside rest stop. It was empty. Farrow parked and we got out into the glaring midday sun. The gravel lot was littered with cigarette butts and the remnants of a shredded tire. A McDonald's wrapper fluttered in the weeds. It could have been any rest stop along any highway. I felt nothing, no rush of emotion, no connection to the surroundings. I wasn't sure what I'd expected—a plaque commemorating the spot where Sarabeth Shepherd had been found alive? A rust-colored stain in the dirt where I'd lain bleeding? I realized, then, why it didn't look familiar. I had never seen this place upright, in full daylight. I'd been on the ground, looking up at the sunrise.

Farrow waited expectantly. "Sorry," I said.

"Let's sit with it a minute." The rotting picnic table swayed back and forth as Farrow sat down on the bench, and I perched gingerly at the edge, watching semis struggle up the steep hill, cars zipping past them. After a while, Farrow let out a sigh. "Nothing?"

I shook my head.

"Hey, it's okay. It was worth a shot." He pointed to a billboard in the distance that read, HEADS UP! LAMBERT'S CAFE, HOME OF THROWED ROLLS. "You hungry?"

"Starving. The last thing I ate was that Mr. Goodbar."

"Well, I guess I owe you a big lunch."

"Yeah," I said. "We'll totally be even after that." He shook his head, a smile emerging, maybe the first real smile I'd seen from him.

When we arrived at Lambert's, there was already a line of people waiting to get in. As soon as we were seated, Farrow got a call and excused himself, leaving me alone to study the menu. All the food was country homestyle. Chicken gizzards, hog jowls, beans with fried bologna, black-eyed peas. The warm, yeasty scent of baking bread took me right back to the Darlings' kitchen. I hadn't been in touch with them since I'd left. I wondered if Sylvie was baking for them now, if my absence had forced my sister to take my place. I imagined Sylvie doing all the things that I had done—smiling when she didn't feel like it, working the farm stand in a stifling, cumbersome dress, scrubbing laundry until her fingers cracked and bled, lying in our upstairs bedroom with its bare walls and empty shelves, wracked with desperation, awaiting her inevitable wedding. I remembered the suffocating feeling of powerlessness when I realized that my life was not my own, that someone else was pulling the strings, and that same feeling, later, when I awoke to a blindfold.

I pulled up the map on my phone to see where we were, scrolled across the wide green swaths of wilderness, the crooked blue fingers of rivers and creeks and endless unmarked acres that could swallow you whole. We weren't far from Wisteria.

Farrow returned in time for the waitress to take our orders, and she brought our iced tea in enormous plastic mugs. A teenage boy wheeled out a cart full of steaming rolls and started chucking them at people. One whizzed past me, bounced off the table, and fell to the floor.

"Seriously?" I said.

Farrow smirked. "Didn't you read the sign? It's the home of

throwed rolls." He snatched one out of the air and handed it to me. It was larger than my fist and slick with melted butter.

"That phone call," he said. "I was able to confirm that Abby's mother was registered for last year's Winter Meeting, so I'm going to pursue that angle, see where it leads."

"Great."

"You looking forward to getting back? Sleeping in your own bed?"

"Actually, I think I'm going to pack when I get home," I said. "I've decided to go to my sister's wedding."

"In Wisteria? What changed your mind?"

"I didn't know if I could do it," I said. "Go back there. But I was thinking about Sylvie, and you and your sister. I don't know whether she wants my help, but I don't want to regret that I didn't try."

"Good luck," he said. "However it turns out, I think you'll be glad you went." The waitress deposited a tub of butter on the table and Farrow pushed it toward me. "Go ahead. While the roll's still hot."

"You want half?"

He started to say no, but I gave him half anyway. "Thanks," he said. "And . . . a word of advice. I know you pay attention to your surroundings and take precautions, but just . . . stay aware. I'm well acquainted with the Clayton County offender map. So many red dots it looks like a case of the measles."

"I'll keep my eyes and ears open," I said. "If I come across any useful information, I'll let you know."

"I'd appreciate it," he said. "I know I promised I'd leave you alone after this, but I'd like for you to stay in touch, if you don't mind, especially while you're in Wisteria. You can call me anytime if you need anything, if something comes up. I've got contacts in the Arkansas Highway Patrol."

Our food arrived, my tray heaped with meat loaf, mashed potatoes and gravy, beans, sliced peaches, stewed tomatoes, fried okra, more than a person could hope to eat in one sitting. Farrow's chicken-fried steak was served in an enormous skillet, still sizzling, with a side of okra and a mound of macaroni the size of a human brain. Hunger made my mouth water, but my stomach felt off. It was the sort of meal my family used to have on Sundays after church, a labor-intensive bounty after a week of bread and beans. I never cooked food like this now that I didn't have to, now that I ate alone.

As I watched Farrow dig into his skillet, I realized that this was the first time a man had taken me out to a restaurant. It was one of the things at the top of my teenage wish list along with getting my ears pierced at a mall. In all the times I had fantasized about it, I'd imagined going to Dairy Queen with Noah Blackburn, or eating at Olive Garden with Jack on our way to prom. I never would have guessed that the first time would be anything like this.

Farrow tore a paper towel from the roll we'd been given in place of napkins and handed it to me before taking one for himself. "What's wrong?" he said.

"Nothing. It's a dumb thing even to be thinking about right now."

"What is it?"

"Just—there're lots of things I haven't done. That I wasn't allowed to do, growing up. So I'd build up this idea of what it would be like when I finally got to do it. Like going out to eat with someone. I always thought it would be on a date."

"Oh." He grimaced. "So this is the first time?"

"Yeah. This is it."

He put his hand over his mouth.

"Are you *laughing*?"

"No. It's not funny." He tried to maintain a sympathetic expression but couldn't keep a straight face. "Nothing's funny about this whole situation—I'm just thinking this must be your nightmare version of a first date."

"Not a total nightmare," I said. "The food's good, at least."

"I'm so sorry." He gave up trying to hold in his laughter, and I rolled my eyes.

"It's fine," I said. "Nothing ever turns out quite like you think."

"Hey," he said. "This doesn't have to count. Just forget it happened. You can have a do-over."

My phone buzzed. A text from Helen, with a picture of her hand holding Gypsy's paw. *Just checking in*, she said. *G & I got manicures! Having a good time?*

I snapped a picture of my overloaded plate and sent it to her. *Yes*, I typed. *So good, I'm not sure when I'll be back. Would you be able to keep Gypsy a while longer?*

She answered right away. *Of course! That food looks divine. So glad you're having fun! Can't wait to hear all about it! ;)*

*Thanks*, I replied. *I owe you.*

A heart popped up, the one with sparkles, followed by a paw print. *Anything for a friend.*

# CHAPTER 14

# SARABETH, THEN

## AGE 17

For once I was grateful when Retta volunteered us to clean up the church basement after Sunday school. Mama had hovered over me all week, crackling with the apprehensive energy of an aura preceding a migraine, busying me with extra chores, like washing the curtains and ironing the boys' work overalls. I had told her, as soon as I got home from the disastrous ride with Jack, that Mrs. Darling was taking the computer to get fixed, so I wouldn't be able to finish my class. She hadn't asked any questions, and she didn't say anything about Mrs. Darling calling, but that didn't mean she hadn't. The dread of not knowing curdled in my gut, giving me a constant stomachache.

Retta and I dragged the metal folding chairs to the storage closet and stacked them, banging them around more than necessary so the adults upstairs could tell we were hard at work.

"I have some news," Retta said, her voice somewhere between a whisper and a squeal.

It was rare for anything to happen that truly qualified as news, though certainly my standards had declined over time. News, to

Retta, usually meant a birth, death, or wedding, and she wouldn't be so giddy about a funeral.

"Somebody getting married?"

"Mm-hm." Retta bobbed her head, a bright pink flush spreading from her cheeks to the tips of her ears. "Guess who?"

"I don't know," I said. "Give me a clue."

"It's me!" she said, flinging her arms around my neck and screeching in my ear.

"Really?" I felt my jaw drop, like in a cartoon, mouth gaping, and was glad she couldn't see my face. I squeezed her tight. There was no reason to be surprised—Retta was a year older than me, and she'd been talking about getting married forever—but still, none of the talk had felt real, not until now.

"I wanted to tell you before you heard it from anyone else. It's Philip Werner," she said, pulling away and grabbing my hands.

I tried to think of something to say, but all I could manage was to repeat his name. "Philip Werner?"

Retta nodded, her eyes bright with tears. Philip was in his twenties, and his first wife and baby had died in childbirth. The most notable thing about him was his pallor—his hair was a colorless blond, his fair skin tinged blue like skim milk. He wasn't unpleasant, though I couldn't imagine Retta picking him if given her choice in a lineup.

She burst into giggles and squeezed my hands. "Can you believe it? It's finally happening. I'm going to be married!"

"I'm so happy for you," I said, knowing that was what she wanted to hear.

"Don't worry," Retta said. "It'll be your turn soon. Maybe we'll both have girls and they'll play dolls together just like we used to."

"Yeah," I said. "Maybe."

"Okay, we'll have plenty of time to talk about the wedding later, so now I want to know what's going on with you."

"Me? Nothing."

"Sarabeth," she chided. "I know you better than that. You're jittery. I thought you were going to wear a hole in the floor, the way you were tapping your foot during the sermon."

"I don't know. Restless, I guess. I'm done with school. I'll be eighteen soon. Trying to figure out what's next."

"I know what you mean," she said. "That was me for the last year, remember? Still lumped in with the children instead of the women, because you're not yet a wife. Just know there's a plan. Pray for patience and trust that God will provide. I was actually thinking today when Pastor Rick gave you that blessing, the way he looked at you, he might have you in his heart for Noah."

"That's not quite what I mean, Retta . . . I don't want to get married, not now anyway. I'm worried—" There was a lull in the chatter overhead, and Retta plugged in the vacuum and switched it on, lest anyone upstairs start to think we were idle.

"What is it?"

"I'm thinking about leaving."

She looked wounded, like I'd slapped her.

"Promise you won't tell."

"Of course not," she said. I could barely hear her over the vacuum. The excitement of her engagement had drained from her face, and I felt guilty for ruining her happy day.

"You won't miss me," I said. "You'll have Philip." She nodded, smiling unconvincingly. Despite her unquestioning embrace of marriage and all it entailed, we both knew her husband wouldn't replace her best friend. She would honor and obey him, hold her tongue and bow her head, cook his meals and bear his children. If she was lucky, she might grow to love him. But I doubted she would tell him all the things she'd told me. She wouldn't share the dark confessions she'd buried in the jars. Retta might not want me to leave, but I could trust her not to tell anyone. She knew how to keep a secret.

# CHAPTER 15

# SARAH, NOW

Melissa frowned when I stepped into her office Monday morning to ask for the week off. I rarely took vacation days, and never more than one at a time.

"Some kind of emergency?" she asked.

"No," I said. "Everything's fine. It's . . . a wedding. A family wedding."

The frown deepened. "Last-minute wedding?"

"Well, no. It's been planned for a while. I'm sorry I didn't give you more notice. I didn't think I was going to go, but now I really need to be there."

She sighed. "I get it. Family's family. Where you going? One of those fancy destination deals?"

"No. Clayton County, Arkansas," I said.

Her eyebrows jumped. "You do know they've got a dozen of the worst puppy mills on the Humane Society's Horrible Hundred list, right? And probably more that aren't even on the radar?"

I nodded. That was exactly why I'd mentioned it. Melissa was part of an activist group that fought to shut down puppy mills. It was her number-one passion project on a long list of animal-related passion projects—a topic guaranteed to distract her from asking any more questions about my trip.

"Listen," she said, digging through her desk drawer and extracting a business card. "You know what to look for, right? You see anything shady, you let me know. Night or day, call me, or call the hotline." She tapped the card and then handed it to me. It said FURRY FRIENDS in bold letters across the top. "We don't have anybody in Clayton County—that place is like a black hole, no offense to your family—but we got people on the Missouri side. You come across one of these operations, we'll get somebody out there, scout it out, get 'em busted."

"Okay," I said, slipping the card into my phone case. "I'll keep my eye out."

"Yeah," she said. "Good. Take pictures if you can, any kind of evidence. And get the coordinates. Some of those roads down there aren't on any kind of map. And keep a low profile—don't want to tip 'em off, or piss 'em off. Get yourself shot."

"Right. Will do. Thanks, Melissa."

"Mm-hm," she said, her attention shifting back to her computer. Her fingers flitted across the keyboard, already moving on to other concerns—a motherless bunny, an abandoned pig, a diabetic cat. Karim lifted his hand in a friendly wave as I walked past the exam room, but I didn't stop to talk to him or anyone else on my way out. No different from any other day.

I called the Darlings and left an awkward message, hoping it was still the right number, asking them to tell my parents that I was coming. Driving into the Ozarks wasn't as overwhelming as I'd thought it would be, having just made the trip with Farrow, though I was still nervous about seeing my family, Sylvie especially. I hoped she had forgiven me for leaving, that she somehow understood. My mother had said in one of her first letters that Sylvie was safer without me there, and I would have done anything to protect my sister, even abandon her. It hadn't occurred to me that Mama might have meant something else — that Sylvie would be safe not from my abductor, but from my influence. In leaving, I had failed to protect her from our mother, who wouldn't repeat the mistakes she'd made raising me.

It probably seemed normal to Sylvie, getting married at sixteen. There were plenty of teenage brides at Holy Rock, and she'd been so young when we switched churches and moved to the farm that she barely remembered how things used to be. I'd tried to give her a window into the outside world, retelling my favorite Disney movies in place of bedtime stories, singing her songs that I had memorized from the radio. I talked about our visits to our grandmother's house before Mama had cut off all contact, how Grams would sip a gin and tonic while we played with her makeup and tried to walk in her high heels. Once, when Grams drained her drink, she'd fished out the bitter wedge of lime and let me have a taste. I wondered if Sylvie remembered any of it now, after five years with no one to remind her.

The hills took on a well-worn familiarity as I crossed the state line into Arkansas and drew close to Wisteria. I noticed shadows moving across the road, quickening as I approached, and my skin crawled as I realized what it was. Tarantulas. Dozens of them. I'd managed to arrive in time for mating season, when they emerged from hiding to wander in unsettling hordes. I tried not to take it as an omen, a sign that I should turn back, that I never should have come.

When I reached the farm, the driveway was blocked by a new

cattle gate, and I was forced to park the car and get out. I stepped carefully, watching for spiders, trying to keep my focus on the gate, but as I unwound the chain that held it closed, my eyes were drawn to the farm stand. It was empty, no produce laid out, no one sitting at the table. Behind it stretched the field of withering corn, where I had run that day. Where he'd caught me. I could feel the cornstalks closing in around me, the man's arms crushing me to his chest, and I gasped like I was suffocating. I clutched the chain, counted the links, measured my breaths. My legs threatened to buckle, my will weakening. I had felt a bit braver after my trip with Farrow, but I wasn't sure that I could go through with this. It was only the thought of Sylvie, the hope that I could save her, take her away from all of this, that made me get back in the car, drive through the gate, and secure the chain behind me.

As I came over the ridge, my old home appeared, tucked into the holler, just as I'd left it. Same plain white farmhouse, the door a dull black, the unadorned porch swept clean, nothing in the yard to indicate a family lived inside. It felt sterile and impersonal in comparison to my neighborhood in St. Agnes, where all the houses displayed cheery fall wreaths and early Halloween decorations, the driveways littered with scooters and soccer balls.

I knocked on the front door and moments later it swung wide and Sylvie let out a gleeful squeal. She grabbed my hands and pulled me inside and we stood face-to-face, staring at each other, breathless. So much changes between the ages of eleven and sixteen, and I'd prepared myself not to recognize her, but it was almost more startling to see that she still looked very much like a child, small and slight, her frame not yet softened with curves. Had she hugged me, I could've easily tucked her under my chin. She wore a navy dress with a full skirt falling to her ankles, her long brown hair spilling over her shoulder in shining waves. A simple band on her ring finger signified that she was spoken for. It looked out of place.

"You came," she said, beaming.

"I wouldn't miss a chance to see you," I said. "I was . . . surprised. By the letter. Mama inviting me."

"I told her it was the only wedding present I wanted, to have you here."

She squeezed my fingers and let go, and I felt dizzy with relief. She was happy to see me. I looked around, but no one else was there. The house was silent.

"Where is everyone?"

"The boys are working," she said. "Mama and Daddy are at the Blackburns'. They'll be back. Come on. Let me get you something to drink." She led me to the kitchen, turned on the tap. The same faded yellow curtain hung in the window over the sink, the wooden cross Eli made at Bible camp still centered on the wall above the dining table. A bowl of potatoes sat on the counter, scrubbed and ready to peel. Sylvie handed me a glass of water. "They were already gone when Tom dropped by this morning to say you were coming. They'll be so excited to see you!"

I wasn't sure they'd be excited, but they would be surprised, at least. "I don't know where to start," I said. "I want to hear everything. How are you? How are you feeling about the wedding?"

"I couldn't be happier," she said. "I've been busy getting things ready. Planning the reception, figuring out the food, working on my dress. And now—everything's perfect." She clutched my arm, the way our mother used to do when she had something important to say. "I'd love it if you'd stand up for me at the ceremony, be my maid of honor."

"Of course, Sylvie. Whatever you want." I choked down some water. "Tell me about . . . your fiancé." I'd been wondering what kind of man my parents had chosen for her, if they had taken her preference into consideration at all, or if it was someone she barely knew, like it had been for me.

"Oh, he's *wonderful*," she said. "I think you know him from church—Noah Blackburn? Pastor Rick's son?"

I nodded, breathing through the sudden sharp pain in my chest, a cold blade sliding between my ribs.

"He's quiet and thoughtful and hardworking. And I couldn't be blessed with better in-laws than the Blackburns. Minnie's been helping with everything. She's a gifted seamstress—I bet she can help whip up a dress for you to wear!"

She sounded so much like Retta, so earnest, so unrelentingly positive. Exactly how she'd been raised to be.

"What are your plans for after you're married? Where will you live?"

"On his family's land, out past the old Drury Mill. They've got more than a thousand acres now, and there's a darling little cabin for Noah and me. The front window looks out over the creek, and there's an apple tree. I'm going to put up applesauce and apple butter, make our own cider. We'll probably have to build a proper house before too long, but the cabin's perfect until we start to outgrow it."

"So you're . . . planning for a family, then?"

"It's in God's hands, of course, but I pray for fruitfulness."

*Fruitfulness.* What sixteen-year-old girl prayed for such a thing? At Sylvie's age, I had struggled not to roll my eyes every time Minnie Blackburn opened her pursed mouth and started preaching about the virtue of fertility to the youth group girls.

"You seem so happy, Sylvie," I said. "But you can be completely honest with me. Is this really what you want?"

"Yes," she said. "I've always wanted to be a wife, a mother. Ever since I was little. You know that. I used to pretend the kittens were my babies, remember?"

I remembered her playing at being a mommy, but I had done the same thing at her age. I hadn't thought it meant anything. "What's the rush? You're so young still. You can take your time. How well do you even know your husband-to-be?"

"I have faith, Sarabeth. I'm ready."

She said it as though it were a matter of practicality, her certainty clear in her eyes and her childlike voice. It was unsettling. I remembered how it felt to be sixteen and have a crush on a boy—on Noah. It was thrilling, consuming. I'd lie in bed at night feverish with fantasies. Sylvie was talking about apple butter and babies.

"Mama thought you might do this." She patted my arm, her touch soft with sympathy. "If you came here to talk me out of it, it's not going to work. I hope you can understand."

I tried to smile, nod. I couldn't bring myself to say yes. She hugged me, her body curled against mine, allowing me, for a moment, to feel close to her again, to pretend she was still the little girl who'd crawl into my bed at night when a storm rolled in and rain hammered the tin roof.

The front door creaked open, and the house filled with the sounds of shuffling boots and hollered greetings before my brothers burst into the kitchen. Eli swept me up in a bear hug while Luke and Paul waited awkwardly and then politely shook my hand. I'd never been close with my little brothers like I was with Eli, maybe because they were younger when things had changed, when the divide between the boys and girls in our house grew more rigid.

"I knew it was you soon as I saw the car outside," Eli said. "I knew you'd come. It's good to see you."

"You, too," I said. "I see you were finally able to grow a beard."

He laughed, stroking his chin. Luke and Paul had beards, too, dark and thick as Eli's. I wouldn't have recognized my younger brothers on the street, and they seemed uncomfortable to be in the same room with me.

My parents walked in then, my father nodding hello, my mother taking in my short hair, the bare skin exposed by my summer dress. She stepped forward and gave me a stiff, perfunctory embrace.

"What a lovely surprise," she said. "I know we all want to catch up, but for now, let's scoot everyone out of the kitchen so I can fix dinner. You too, Sylvie. Sarabeth can help me, and we can have a bit of mother-daughter time."

When they had all filed out, my mother handed me an apron. "You still remember how to peel potatoes?"

"Of course," I said. I tied the apron around my waist and found the peeler in the same drawer it had been in the last time I'd used it.

"I know I should have written back sooner, to let you know I was coming. I called the Darlings to tell you."

"I'm sure Sylvie was pleased to see you."

"Thank you for letting me come."

"This is your home," she said. "We are your family. You're always welcome here."

She got butter out of the fridge to soften. I noticed silver hairs creeping up from the nape of her neck and thought of Grams, how Mama had let her own mother die alone in a nursing home because they had fought over our increasingly uncompromising lifestyle.

"Do you mean that?"

She slapped the butter dish down on the counter.

"Do you know what happened when you left?" she hissed. "A social worker came to the house. Someone from the department of family services. They were *concerned* about our children for some reason. They wanted to interview them without us present. It was humiliating. Your sister was terrified. She cried for a week."

"I'm sorry. I didn't know."

"You didn't know? Really? Why do you think they came? Why do you think they suddenly wanted to investigate our children's well-being?"

I clutched the peeler, the dull blade biting into my palm. She blamed me.

"Your father's never gotten over it. Sylvie was heartbroken. You didn't even tell her goodbye." She pushed up her sleeves, washed her hands in cold water. "But despite all that, yes, you are welcome here. You are one of our flock. We pray for your soul every day. Especially your sister."

I remembered the game we played at Bible camp, how Sylvie would cry for every soul she failed to save. I had come home in hopes of rescuing her, but she didn't want my help. I wondered if she'd invited me back because the fate of my soul weighed on her, if she thought I was the one who needed saving.

· · ·

I felt like an unwelcome ghost at the dinner table, my parents and younger brothers doing their best not to look at me. The conversation was stilted at first, Daddy talking at length about the weather. Finally Eli told a funny story about a temperamental cow that had been found wandering the Price Chopper parking lot, and everyone cracked up, even Mama. When the laughter died down, they seemed more relaxed and began to chat with one another about everyday things I had no part of, as though they'd forgotten I was there. My family had knitted back together without me, my absence a wound that had healed over and left no visible scar.

Afterward, we gathered together in the living room to sing hymns, a tradition Mama had started when we moved to the farm. To me, it had served as a bitter reminder that we no longer had a TV to watch or books to read. I hadn't sung in years, but the verses flowed out of me from memory, unbidden. *In life, in death, O Lord, abide with me!* It was disorienting, my mouth forming words I thought I'd forgotten. The room grew steadily darker as the sun went down. I watched them sing, their faces shadowed and unfamiliar in the dying light. They were my blood, but they were strangers. It felt wrong to be here. Beneath the joyful music, tension threaded through me like a trip wire.

# CHAPTER 16

# SARABETH, THEN

## AGE 17

My legs cramped as I attempted to get up from the floor. I'd finally finished scrubbing all the cabinets and baseboards in the kitchen. Mama had been finding all sorts of indoor tasks to keep me busy and within her line of sight. Anytime I left the house, she made sure Sylvie went with me.

"Retta's wedding will be here before we know it," Mama said. She was seated at the kitchen table, flipping through her prayer journal. "If you're planning to sew a new dress, you'd best get started."

I couldn't keep my eyes from rolling. I wasn't about to sew anything, even for Retta. It didn't matter what I wore, whether it was old or new. Every dress was the same: long skirt, long sleeves, plain fabric, blah, blah, blah.

"No need to be fancy," I said, wringing out my cleaning rag in the sink. "I'll just wear something I already have." It was exactly the kind of thing she would say herself, and I figured she'd be pleased to think her humble practicality had finally rubbed off on me. Pleased enough that she'd shut up about sewing.

"But you want to look *nice*," she said. "A wedding is a special occasion. You should wear your hair down, maybe curl it a little."

"The day's all about the bride," I said, pouring on the humility. "It doesn't matter how I look."

"It's not *all* about the bride," she said, a coy smile emerging. "It's a social event as well. You want to make a good impression." She smoothed her apron. "I was speaking to Donna Hartzell this afternoon, and she said that Doug is building a house on their land."

Doug was several years older and worked at his father's sawmill. A while back, he had accidentally sawn off two of his fingers. We had taken cinnamon rolls to his family at church, and that was the only time I could remember speaking to him directly. *Sorry about your fingers*, I'd said. My mother had pinched the back of my arm, twisting the flesh tight until I added that we were praying for him.

"That's nice," I said, edging toward the stairs. I wondered if she'd believe me if I said I needed to go to my room and work on a Sunday school assignment. Now that I'd finished my homeschooling, it was getting harder to find excuses to be left alone. Mama was constantly on alert for idleness.

"He'll be looking for a wife soon, I imagine, once the house is done." She eyed me meaningfully. "He'll make a good husband for someone."

"I'm sure he will."

"He'd make a good husband for *you*." She clasped her hands over her heart and beamed at me, as though marrying an eight-fingered stranger was the most wonderful thing she could wish for me. I had almost made it to the staircase. I could mumble something pleasant but noncommittal, nod politely, escape to my room. It would only make things worse if I argued with her,

and things were bad enough already. *Nod*, I told myself. *Smile.*
But I couldn't do it.

"What makes you think that?" I said. "I don't even know him.
I know nothing about him except that he's not very careful with
a saw."

The joy drained from her face, replaced by a look of bitter
determination. "You ungrateful child," she said. "I'm trying to
help you. You don't understand what your father and I have done
for this family, what we've given you. Your father quit his job, we
moved to this farm, to create a better life for our children. For
*you*."

"Really? I thought it was because Daddy screwed a waitress."

"*Sarabeth*." Her low voice dripped venom.

"Do you think any of us believe we moved out here and left
our whole lives behind because he had *impure thoughts*? How
did you find out about her? Were there pictures on his phone?
Did he tell you what they did together?"

Her face reddened, her jaw clenching. It felt good to make
her angry. Like I was the one in control.

"That is *enough*, Sarabeth."

"I can see why he did it," I said. "I don't blame him."

She grabbed my arm and twisted. "You get down on your
knees and start praying."

I thought of everything she had taken from me. My friends.
My books. My clothes. Music. Movies. Dancing. School. She
dictated every tiny piece of my life, made every decision for me.
And now she was telling me who to marry. I was sick of her telling me what to do.

"You can fuck off," I said.

She whipped her hand back to slap me, pausing for a moment for dramatic effect, and I slapped her first, as hard as I could.

She gaped at me with horror, one hand on her face and the other clutching her belly, as though shocked that such a devil-child could have sprung from her own womb. I turned to climb the stairs and she didn't try to stop me. I lay on my bed, my heart thudding like I'd been running through the fields, wondering how many lashes I'd earned, whether I could keep from crying out when the belt split my skin. I might get something worse than the belt this time, but I didn't care.

My anger hadn't subsided, even after the slap. The *Guide for Godly Girls* that Mama had so carefully made for me sat on my shelf, the flowered cover faded and coated with dust. I opened it up to the first page and started scribbling over the top of Mama's perfect handwriting. I wrote 666, the number of the Beast, and then I scrawled it again and again, filling lines, margins, pages, the pen scratching through the paper, knowing what it would do to my mother when she found it. When we lived in town, she would cross the street to avoid walking by a house with the Devil's number.

Twenty minutes passed until Mama opened the door without knocking.

"Pastor Rick is here to see you."

"What for? An exorcism?"

The pastor emerged from behind my mother, filling up the doorway. "Hello, Sarabeth." I jolted to my feet. He came in and shut the door behind him, leaving Mama in the hallway. "It's okay," he said. "I'm just here to talk. Your family's worried about you."

I didn't say anything. He came closer, close enough that he could have reached out and touched me, but he didn't. Instead, he sat down on Sylvie's bed, facing me. "Have a seat," he said.

I sat at the edge of my bed, my hands planted at my sides,

wishing I could push myself up off the yellow blanket and run out the door.

"I hear you've been having some trouble lately," he said, leaning forward. "And I want you to know that I can help. We can talk through some things, you and me."

"I don't need to talk," I said. "I'm fine."

"Your mother would disagree." He smiled, his teeth gleaming. "Look, I was a teenager once. There's no need to be embarrassed about anything. It's a confusing time. So much is changing, so many emotions. Sometimes it's easier to talk to someone aside from your parents. I know at church, I'm usually the one doing all the talking, but if you give me a chance, I think you'll see I'm a really good listener."

"Thank you for the offer," I said, hoping that would be sufficient to get him to leave. It wasn't. We stared at each other until I gave up and dropped my gaze. Dark chest hair sprouted from the open collar of his shirt. He wore all black, like a priest.

"I'll let your mother know you didn't feel like talking today," he said finally, smoothing his hand over Sylvie's blanket. He heaved himself up from the bed, leaving a dent in the thin mattress, and clasped my shoulder, his hand like a vise. "I'll be waiting when you change your mind."

# CHAPTER 17

# SARAH, NOW

I had dreaded climbing into my childhood bed and sleeping in the claustrophobic room under the eaves. I was grateful that Sylvie fell asleep immediately, that she didn't see me checking and double-checking the window, panicking when I remembered that the door didn't have a lock. I had brought my nightlight but the only outlet was on Sylvie's side, and I couldn't decide whether or not to plug it in. I fell asleep with it in my hand, eyes on the door, counting my breaths. If I had nightmares I didn't remember them.

I spent my first full day on the farm helping Sylvie with chores and wedding preparations while Mama worked to finish the double wedding ring quilt she was making for Sylvie and Noah. I recognized the fabric. She'd started piecing it together before I left home. It had originally been meant for me.

Sylvie praised the Lord for the beautiful weather, sang as we mucked out the chicken coop, smiled serenely while crafting handmade place cards with the same perfect handwriting as our mother. I kept waiting for her to break character, to say or do something that might hint at a different Sylvie underneath, a slightly less agreeable one.

"Here you go," she said, holding up the card she'd carefully lettered with my name. *Sarabeth.* No one here called me Sarah. Maybe I hadn't told them, though I doubted it would have mattered. I would always be Sarabeth here. Something twisted inside of me every time I heard my old name spoken aloud. "Let's see yours," Sylvie said.

She had let me do Eli's, the one with the fewest letters. The *E* started out fine, but the *l* and the *i* had looked too skinny, so I'd tried to fatten them up and it got worse from there. Sylvie tried not to grimace. "Sorry," I said. "I'll redo it."

"It's okay," she said, giggling. "Eli won't mind." She added it to the stack and started on the next card, Mama's.

"Sylvie . . . I know you're sure that you're ready to get married. But how do you *know* you're sure? You've barely left the farm. You haven't had a chance to experience anything else. Don't you want to see what's out there before you decide what to do with the rest of your life?"

She folded her hands, tilted her head thoughtfully. "You grew up here, too, and somehow you knew you wanted something else, even though you'd never seen it."

"That's not really true. I had a glimpse of it, at least. Before we moved, I had TV, books, the internet, friends from school. You didn't have any of that."

"Yes, and I'm grateful to Mama and Daddy for keeping me away from it. I like how simple things are here. I can focus on my family and my faith, the things that are truly important. I loved growing up on the farm, and I want to raise my children the same way." She reached out and took my hand. "You loved the farm, too," she said. "I know you did. Don't you miss home, at least a little?"

"I miss *you*," I said. I could feel her slipping away from me even as I held her hand. Her whole world was in Wisteria. She didn't want to leave. She smiled, and we got back to our work.

I was so focused on Sylvie that I had to remind myself she wasn't the only reason I was here. I'd promised Farrow that I'd let him know if I came across anything that might connect back to Abby and Destiny. The least I could do was ask around, see what people were saying, and the one person I had always counted on for gossip was Retta. When Sylvie and I finished the place cards, I got Retta's number from Mama, and once I worked up the nerve to call, she invited me to stop by for a visit after supper.

Retta and Philip's property stood out from the others on the long dirt road past Bethel Church. There were no rusting appliances, roaming dogs, or NO TRESPASSING signs. The yard was tidy, almost barren. A split-rail fence bordered the road, and all vegetation had been scalped close to the dirt, except for a pair of withered rosebushes on either side of the front step, the leaves skeletonized by insects. The modest house was clad in rustic Ozark field rock, the stones pieced together like a puzzle, mortar crumbling in between. Retta whipped the door open before I could finish knocking. She wore a long pink dress buttoned up to the neck, her hair piled high on her head in an old-fashioned Gibson Girl bun.

"Sarabeth!" She stood in the doorway for a moment, blinking, and then scooted aside so I could pass through. "Come in."

The cramped living room was dated but well cared for, the

flowered curtains starched and ironed, shabby furniture draped with pretty hand-knit afghans, the tired orange carpet bearing fresh vacuum lines. There were no toys or sippy cups or any other sign of children, and I wondered if there had been a problem, because she had wanted to start having babies right away. Or at least she had the last time I'd spoken to her.

"Philip's at work," she said, leading me to the couch to sit down. "And the boys are already in bed, or I'd introduce them."

"Boys, plural?" I said. "Congratulations! How many?"

"Three, so far," she said. "We're so blessed. They're all healthy. All miniature Philips, blond and fair and serious, just like him. You wouldn't know I was involved, from looking at them." She pressed one hand to her belly, and I could see the protrusion beneath her dress. "I'd love to have a little girl, if God sees fit. Remember how much fun we used to have, playing dolls? We thought our own daughters would play together one day."

"Yeah," I said. "It doesn't seem like that long ago." We were practically still playing with dolls when she got engaged. And now she had three kids of her own, maybe another on the way. This could have been my life, too, if I hadn't been taken, if that hadn't changed everything. I didn't like to think of my abduction having a silver lining, but I wondered, if I had been given a choice back then—to stay and get married, or endure that horrific week with a promise of freedom—which one I would have chosen.

"How are you?" I asked. "I feel like I've missed so much. The wedding, the babies . . . I can't believe you're a mom! What's it like—married life, Philip, all of it?"

"It's everything I prayed for," she said. "Philip . . . I'm so lucky. He's a good man, Sarabeth, he really is. He's kind. He's patient. He's a good father. He always compliments my cooking, even when it's awful." The giggle returned, the one that used to punctuate every sentence when we were kids, and a genuine smile warmed her face. She was still the Retta I knew, still my friend, despite all that had changed.

"I'm happy for you."

She shook her head. "I can't believe it sometimes. I barely get a moment's rest with three little ones, but I wouldn't have it any other way."

I hoped she truly was as happy as she was trying to make it seem. My boss, Melissa, was always rolling her eyes at her ex's Facebook page, claiming that the people bragging about how happy they are, the ones who really shove it in your face, are all miserable on the inside, their smiles just for display.

"What's it like for you?" Retta's smile faded. "Out there? I've thought of you so many times, prayed for you. I felt awful that you had to leave all on your own."

She made it sound like I'd been exiled to outer space. "I wasn't really alone," I said. "I had people helping me. I have a job now, a house. I'm doing fine."

"But you're not married yet?" She gestured to my ringless hand. "Are you . . . dating someone?"

"No. I'm busy with work, and . . . other things."

"Do you go roller-skating?"

"What?"

Retta looked down at her lap, embarrassed by my reaction. "You always talked about how you missed it. How your friends were probably skating without you on Friday nights while you were stuck at home."

"Oh, yeah. I think I'm too old now. It'd be weird, someone my age going to a skating rink alone."

"Of course," she said. "Sorry, that was dumb. I guess I just imagined you doing all the things you couldn't do here—getting your ears pierced, going to the movies."

"It's not dumb," I said. "Things are just different than I thought they'd be, I guess."

She nodded, smoothing her skirt over her lap. "I thought of you," she said. "When I heard about Noah and Sylvie. I know you cared for him. I worried it might be hard for you."

"No. I mean . . . I didn't expect that Sylvie would be getting married so soon. And I didn't expect it to be him. But Noah and I were never going to end up together. Before I left, my mother was trying to marry me off to Doug Hartzell. We got in a huge fight over it."

"I need to tell you something," Retta blurted.

"What?"

"It was my fault, I think, that your mother was keeping such a close eye on you, right before you went missing. That she was in such a rush for you to marry Doug. I told her you were planning to leave. I prayed on it, and I truly believed it was the right thing to do. But then, everything that happened, after . . . I felt like it was my fault in a way, like one thing led to another. That maybe none of it would have gone like it did if I hadn't said anything."

I wasn't sure what to say. It had never occurred to me that Retta would have told my parents anything. It probably hadn't made a difference, because my mother was upset about my attitude anyway, but it might have helped explain why they assumed I'd run away, why they hadn't called the police when I disappeared. Retta looked ready to cry, her face all crinkled up.

"Forget it," I said. "It doesn't matter now."

"It was selfish of me," she said. "I didn't want you to leave. We always talked about the things we'd do together. I wanted you to stay here with me, but nothing worked out the way I thought it would. You left just the same."

"I didn't want to leave you, Retta, but you were happy here — you were getting married, and that was all you ever wanted. I didn't want any of that. The only way out of it was to leave. And then after what happened, I couldn't stay."

"I know," Retta said. "And I'm so sorry. Please don't hate me."

"I don't hate you." I reached out to squeeze her hand. "It was a long time ago. I'm glad to see you, I really am. I've missed you."

A wan smile crossed her face. "I've missed you, too. You have no idea. I have Philip, and my family, and the women's group . . . but no one took your place. There's no one I can talk to the way we used to."

"I thought about writing to you," I said. "But I didn't know if you'd want to hear from me. When I was home, after they found me . . . you never called or came by."

"I wanted to," she said. "But my parents wouldn't let me. I helped my mother make meals to take to your family. I prayed so hard. I couldn't imagine what you'd been through. And I actually did write you a letter," she said. "Telling you all the things I didn't get to say. I buried it, so my mother wouldn't see. Old habits."

"What did you think had happened?" I said. "What did they tell you?"

"I didn't know you'd been gone until you were back. Your family wasn't at church because Sylvie'd been so sick and I figured you were sick, too, or helping take care of her. There was no talk until after, and then people said you'd run away and gotten yourself into trouble."

"So no one believed my side of the story?"

She shrugged. "Maybe they didn't even hear it. They don't trust the news. They make up their own minds. It doesn't matter what they think."

"What about you?"

"You remember when I told you about what had happened to me? About Leon? You never asked if I was making it up. You didn't ask me a bunch of questions to see if all the pieces fit together, if they made sense. You just believed me. You were my best friend. And I know you're not a liar."

I exhaled with relief. I hadn't realized how badly I'd still wanted—needed—Retta to believe me. "Do you ever wonder, since they never figured out who did it, if he's still out there? That was another reason I wanted to leave. I worried that he'd come back, or that he was here, right in front of us. Have you noticed anything strange around Wisteria since I've been gone? Anything out of the ordinary? Anyone acting differently?"

Retta looked down at her chapped hands, and I imagined the work they endured each day. Scrubbing diapers, washing dishes, cleaning up every crumb and smear and fingerprint left behind by three small children. An oppressive silence swelled to fill the room. There were none of the sounds I'd grown used to from living in town, no traffic, no neighbors. Not a whisper of breath from her sleeping sons.

"Retta?"

She got up and went to the door, peeking through the curtain as if to make certain no one was outside. It was getting dark.

"Philip will be home soon," she said.

"Do you want me to go? Would he not want me to be here?"

"No," she said, shaking her head. "It's not that. He just . . . doesn't like gossip. He finds it unbecoming of a lady." She sat back down. "This might not be anything. There was a new girl at church, younger than us . . . I didn't know her very well, except she helped out with the preschoolers quite a bit. My nieces just adored her. But she tried to run away, for real. Took her parents' car. Didn't make it out of the county, though—she didn't have a license, never learned how to drive. Wound up in a ditch. I heard Pastor Rick helped her parents send her on a mission trip somewhere, to get her straightened out."

"And you think that might be connected somehow?"

"Well, not that part, but there was something else. A rumor. That she was pregnant. Supposedly somebody who worked at the clinic was there when she was brought in after the accident, and they overheard the nurse. I don't know if that was true, or just talk. But I wondered, if she really was pregnant, who had done that to her, and if it might have been the same man. The one who took you."

"Oh." It was a stretch. Even if the rumor was true and the girl was pregnant, it didn't necessarily indicate a crime. It was impossible to know without digging deeper, but Farrow had said any piece of information could be important, that leads might come from unexpected places. "What's her name?"

"Eva Winters. A tiny little thing with dark hair and freckles. She really took to missionary work. She's not back yet." She looked up at me. "Do you think you'll ever come back? Not just for a visit, but for good?"

"I don't think so," I said. "But that doesn't mean we can't stay in touch. We can write letters, talk on the phone. We don't have to let five more years go by."

"If you change your mind," she said, "it's never too late to come home."

Retta promised, when I left, that I'd see her and Philip and the boys at Sylvie's wedding. It had grown dark outside, darker than it ever got in St. Agnes, with its porch lights and streetlights and the hazy glow of the city. I hurried to the car and tried to text Farrow to tell him about the other girl, Eva Winters, but the message wouldn't go through, so I tried calling instead. The phone rang and rang as I crossed the low-water bridge and made my way out of the holler, my headlights reflecting the glowing eyes of hidden creatures at the edge of the woods. It didn't seem like Farrow not to answer right away. I left him a voicemail, wondering what he was doing, what kept him away from the phone.

# CHAPTER 18

# SARABETH, THEN

### AGE 17

I sucked in a panicked breath and choked, the fear of suffocation overwhelming as I woke to absolute darkness, a cloth covering my face and sticking to my crusted mouth. I coughed and struggled but could barely move. The last thing I remembered was the sun spilling down through the corn, the man in the mask holding me against his chest, covering my mouth as I screamed. My heart clutched into a fist, squeezing tighter and tighter until I thought it would burst, but minutes passed and it continued to beat, just as air moved in and out of my lungs, stale and humid and sustaining. Once I convinced myself that I could breathe, that I would not die in that moment or the next, my mind scurried to other fears, racing into the darkest corners. I didn't know where I was or what was going to happen to me. I wasn't sure how long I'd been there, whether it was night or day. Beyond the blindfold, I imagined the darkness pressing down on me, layer upon layer, a windowless room buried underground beneath a black, moonless sky, miles of emptiness void of electric light.

Amid the panic, one small mercy rose to the surface, and I

clung to it. Wherever I was, for the moment at least, I was alone. I didn't sense anyone else in the room. If I was going to try to get out, I needed to do it before the man returned. My back pressed against a stone or concrete wall, my arms spread to either side crucifixion style, wrists bound to an unmoving object, maybe a pipe, fingers half numb. I twisted my neck from side to side, the muscles kinked and aching. I tried to rub my face against my arm to loosen the blindfold, but it was tight, entangled in my hair, and there was some sort of loose sack over that, which seemed to be fastened at the neck. My dress had ridden up and I could feel a rough blanket or canvas tarp beneath my bare thighs. The space around me felt small and enclosed and slightly damp. A cellar maybe, or a crawl space. I stretched my legs out as far as I could without wrenching my arms out of their sockets, my bare feet encountering nothing but the blanket and the floor. My ankles were shackled together, with some sort of bar between them.

I tested my voice, and it was hoarse. I had the feeling that screaming wouldn't help anyway. I scooted my bottom back against the wall to relieve the strain in my neck and shoulders and folded my legs beneath my dress as best I could. I was alive. That didn't mean he wouldn't kill me, but I was alive for now, for some reason, and that reason couldn't be good.

I tried to remember him. Everything had happened so quickly that some details were blurred. He wore a hat and mask, but I couldn't recall his clothing. He hadn't spoken, or shown his face, or reached for the cash box. He was strong, had caught me easily and held me tight as I fought.

All I could do was wait in the dark, in the thick silence. My instinct was to pray, though I hadn't prayed in earnest, with the hope that it would do any good, in years. None of my prayers had ever been answered the way that I wanted. My mother tried to explain the difference between wishing and praying, and Pastor Rick preached about God's divine wisdom exceeding our human understanding, but I figured if God was going to do what He wanted regardless, there was no point in trying to sway Him.

I'd joined the church prayer circle in praying for the Hannemeyers' little boy when he got sick, and he'd gotten worse and died. The Hannemeyers had accepted God's will that Josiah not live to see his second birthday, comforted by faith that they would see him again in Heaven. I couldn't believe that in a Heaven already teeming with little boys, God needed this particular one, Josiah Hannemeyer of Wisteria, Arkansas, who had only recently learned to walk. Still, there were flickers of uncertainty, that maybe I hadn't prayed hard enough, that I wasn't doing it right, that I was failing some test God had placed before me. If prayer did work, I had to believe that my mother prayed more than enough to make up for my lapses. She'd been praying overtime lately, trying to get me back on what she felt was the right path, and she would surely be praying when she discovered that I was missing. I hoped, though, that my parents wouldn't rely on God's will to bring me home, that they would also call the sheriff.

I rested my head against the wall and thought of Sylvie, who had been so sick that she hadn't said goodbye when I left the house. Maybe her illness did serve a divine purpose, just as Mama had said. Maybe God had spared her by keeping her from going with me. And if God had protected Sylvie, I had to consider that he was punishing me, for my sharp tongue or my lack of faith or any number of sins and shortcomings, or perhaps at the behest of my mother's fervent prayers.

# CHAPTER 19

# SARAH, NOW

The morning after my visit with Retta, I woke at dawn to feed the chickens with Sylvie and then excused myself to take a walk while she and Mama did their Bible study. Mama raised an eyebrow but didn't say a word. It seemed like she'd said all she wanted to say to me the night I arrived, and now she was biting her tongue and silently counting the hours until I was gone.

I walked up the hill through the dew-covered grass toward the Darlings' farm. The house came into view, and then the big red barn, and out front a lone figure kneeling to examine a tractor tire. I wasn't sure that I intended to go closer until I did.

A coonhound emerged from the shade of the barn and began to bark, his snout pitching upward. The man looked up, and after a pause, his arm rose in an uncertain wave. He adjusted his baseball cap and walked toward me. The dog reached me first, and I bent down, palm outstretched for him to sniff. He licked my hand, tail wagging.

"That you, Sarabeth?"

"Hi, Tom." He looked almost rugged, which I never would

have imagined, his gangly frame filled out, his face deeply tanned
from working outdoors, his jaw bearing a hint of stubble. "Good
to see you."

He smiled, the same warm smile that had always broken out
when Eli and I came over. "You look different," he said. "Good,
I mean. Your hair . . ."

My hand instinctively went to my shoulder, where I sometimes felt the weight of my missing hair, like a phantom limb. "I
feel lighter without it."

He nodded. "Yeah. It suits you."

"Looks like you kept growing after I left."

He laughed. "That's fair. Guess I did. Takes a bit of muscle to
keep this place going."

"You're . . . farming now?"

He pulled up his shirtsleeve to reveal the telltale line where
his skin turned from dark to light. "Got a real farmer's tan and
everything."

"You're fully committed."

"Yeah, well. What else was I gonna do. So . . . you're back for
the wedding."

"Mm-hm."

"I bet Sylvie's real happy you could make it."

"I think so," I said. "Not so sure about everybody else."

"Ah." He didn't look surprised. "You got time to stay and visit
a minute? I could get you some coffee. Or a Coke, like old times."

"Coffee would be great, thanks. And I'd love to say hi to your
grandparents, if they're home?"

"They're not, unfortunately," he said. "Gramma got a new
hip and had some complications from surgery, so she's recovering at a nursing home. She doesn't like me to call it a home,
though, because she doesn't plan to stay long. But Grampa's with

her, so at least she's not alone. They'll be real sorry they missed you."

We walked to the house and went in through the kitchen door, like I used to when I baked for Mrs. Darling. Tom made coffee with the old percolator and we sat together at the kitchen table, the dog at our feet.

"They worried about you," Tom said. "We all did. Wondered how you were doing. But your parents acted like you fell off the face of the earth. We didn't have any way to reach you. Gramma kept hoping you'd write or call."

"Yeah. It took me a long time before I could even write to my family. I just wanted to leave everything behind, you know? Start fresh."

"I get it," he said. "And I don't blame you. I can't imagine what you went through. I hope things are better now? That you're doing all right? I don't want to pry. I'm sure you're already sick of people asking you questions."

"No, it's fine. There's not much to tell. The biggest change is probably just all the little things. I can wear pants now. Watch TV. Drive."

"I remember us driving around in the Gator," he said. "Pretending we were out cruising like the cool kids."

"That was fun," I said. "Some of the best times I had here were with you."

"It's hard, I bet, to be back."

"Yeah," I said. "It is. But it's not all bad. I get to see my family. Retta. You. What have you been up to?"

He gestured toward the window, the fields beyond. "Just . . . this. The farm. I don't get out much, and there's nothing to do anyway. Everybody our age is married or in jail or working, trying to get by. I'm this close to turning into one of those creepy old guys who buys beer for high school kids so they'll hang out with him."

"I doubt that," I said. "What about Jack? Is he still around?"

"Jack? He went away to college, came back with a pregnant girlfriend, now he's assistant manager at Price Chopper. Everett went to school with him but got in some trouble and dropped out partway through. Works at his dad's car wash in town."

"What kind of trouble?"

"I don't know. All I heard was he got arrested."

"Do you and Eli ever hang out? I've barely seen him since I got back. Haven't had a chance to catch up."

He looked down at his coffee cup. "Nah. Haven't seen much of him since you left, really. Think it made him uncomfortable, being here without you. He might've caught on that I had a bit of a crush."

"On Eli?"

"That bother you?"

"No, I just . . . I kissed you that time. When we were watching *Little House*."

He laughed. "I remember."

"I'm sorry. I didn't know. You could have told me."

"No, I couldn't," he said. "You know what it's like around here. This isn't the kind of place where you want to stand out."

"There's life outside Wisteria. You don't have to stick around here."

"Not forever, maybe," he said. "But till my grandparents are gone. I wouldn't trust Ronnie to look after them, or the farm."

"Ronnie's still here?"

"Oh, yeah. I thought we'd be rid of him for a while when he stole a car, but he claimed it was all a misunderstanding—everything's a misunderstanding with him. Spent less than a year locked up and came out saved. Found Jesus at the Clayton County Jail."

"Really?"

"Yeah. Pastor Blackburn visits the inmates as part of his ministry. Ronnie latched on to that, cleaned himself up, took some computer classes, got a shortened sentence. Blackburn gave him a job when he got out and everything. Not sure I buy the act, but we'll see how long he can keep it up."

"When did he get out?"

"Seven, eight months ago."

"Is he staying here?"

"Nah, Grampa didn't want him in the house. Got him set up in a trailer on Blackburn's land."

Tom laced his fingers together the way I used to do for Sylvie when she was little. *Here's the church, here's the steeple, open the doors and see all the people.*

"You know," he said, "I always felt like things turned sour after he showed up here. But I think I liked it better when he wasn't pretending to be something he's not. You knew what to expect. Now I've got no idea what he's up to." He sipped his coffee, spooned in more sugar from the flowered sugar bowl at the center of the table.

"What kind of work does Ronnie do for the Blackburns?"

"Website stuff, mostly, but he helps out at the kennels. They sell hunting dogs now." He peeked under the table at the sleeping dog. "That's where I got Ralph. He's no good at hunting, but that's all right. Keeps me company."

"Will you be at the wedding?"

"Nah." He smiled wryly. "Be kind of awkward going alone. But if you need a break from your family, come on over and see me. We could resurrect Secret Thursday. Watch some *Little House* on TV. Hell, I'd even let you kiss me for old times' sake."

We laughed like we had as kids, when we would do stupid things for fun, back before Ronnie showed up. I had felt at home in this kitchen with Tom. We'd been there for each other when each of us had been in desperate need of a friend. We'd talked about the future, how different it would be, though things hadn't turned out quite like we'd expected. Both of us were still on the outside of the lives we wanted to live, holding back in our own ways, for our own reasons. He was stuck here, partly out of obligation, maybe partly because he was scared to leave.

"This house was a refuge to me," I said. "And my house is always open to you. I mean it." I got up to hug him, squeezing tight. "If you ever get out of Wisteria," I said, "you come see me."


On the way home from Tom's, I walked up the road until I got cell service and called Farrow. This time, he picked up immediately.

"Everything all right?"

"Yeah," I said. I heard him exhale.

"Good," he said. "What's up?"

"Possible leads." The words sounded ridiculous coming out of my mouth, like I was playing at being a detective, which I guess I was. "Ronnie Darling. Our neighbor's cousin. He lived with them for a while, back when I was working at their house. Apparently he spent some time in jail after I left and got out less than a year before Abby disappeared."

"Got it. I'll check it out. Anything else?"

"Maybe. The boys from town we talked about. One of

them . . . Everett Linley. He got into some trouble at college and moved back home. I don't know what he did, or how useful that is, but I figured you might want to look into it."

"No, that's great. I really appreciate it. I'll start digging. You never know." He sounded tired. Exhausted.

"How are you doing?"

"I'm fine," he said. "Don't worry about me. You feel safe there? Things all right with your family?"

"Yeah. It's good."

"Glad to hear that," he said.

"Any news on Destiny?"

"They're sifting through hours of footage from hunting cameras in the surrounding areas. Nothing but deer and possums so far. I'll let you know if anything changes. In the meantime, keep in touch. I'll take any leads you've got."

"Wait—did you get my message from last night? About the girl from Wisteria?"

"Oh, yeah. Thanks for that. I did a quick search and didn't come up with anything on Eva Winters. Literally nothing. But that's not unheard-of. Some of these more isolated families do their best to stay off the grid—unregistered home births, never enrolled in school, no vaccinations, no driver's license. Makes them hard to track. I'll have to do a deeper dive. How much longer will you be down there?"

"Few more days. Wedding's Sunday afternoon. I'll leave that night."

"I guess I might be joining you."

"Joining me?" I had a fleeting vision of Farrow escorting me to the wedding, meeting my parents, posing as my boyfriend, everything going horribly awry, like a scene from a romantic comedy.

"If any of these leads show promise, I might have to head down there myself. I'll let you know."

When I got back to the house, I found Sylvie in our bedroom, all the clothes from my bag spread out across her bed. I'd packed the three most modest dresses I owned—frumpy hand-me-downs from my time at the women's shelter—in an effort to appease my family. "What are you doing, Syl?"

She smiled sweetly. "I'm unpacking for you! You can't live out of a bag. I was worried your things'd get wrinkled. Which of these dresses were you planning to wear to the wedding?"

"The nice one." I pointed to the dress with the longest skirt, a loose flowered maxi that I'd never worn.

Sylvie twisted up her mouth. "I bet it looks so pretty on you," she said. "But it's rather . . . bright. Would you consider something closer to my colors, since you're my maid of honor now?" She clasped her hands together. "Minnie already volunteered to make you one like hers."

"That sounds like too much trouble. The wedding's in four days."

"She already has the pattern and the fabric. Please, sis. I'd feel rude saying no."

"Uh . . . if it really means that much to you, I guess."

"Thank you, Sarabeth!" she squealed. "We should head over there now, so she can measure you and get started. Mama already said it was okay for me to ride with you."

In the car, Sylvie asked me to put on the gospel station, but I couldn't find it, so I turned the radio off. She navigated, cheerily narrating the scenery along the way. *This is the bridge that got swept away in the spring flood. That's what's left of the Hannemey-*

ers' place that burned down. There's a tree growing inside the old stone silo! See the leaves poking out the top?

I didn't care what I wore to the wedding. I'd only agreed to the new dress to make Sylvie happy. I hadn't been thinking about what it would entail, the time I'd have to spend with Minnie Blackburn. The farther we got from home, the deeper we drove into the hills, the more I wanted to turn around.

# CHAPTER 20

# SARABETH, THEN

## AGE 17

In my dream, a door opened, and I woke with a start, gasping, still in the dark. Someone was in the room with me, a presence looming in the small space. My heart seized up and then began to beat with such force that my entire body seemed to move with it, rocking forward and back. There was rustling as things were set down on the floor, and then the bag was untied and removed from my head. The blindfold remained in place.

Something was pressed to my open mouth and I jerked away, liquid spilling over my lips and down my chest. My tongue darted to taste it and I was given another drink, the water fresh and cold. A chunk of bread followed, and another, alternating with sips of water, and it occurred to me that if he planned to kill me right away, he wouldn't bother to feed me. It was a small comfort, because I knew nothing good would happen to me in this room, but it allowed me to shove the fear aside enough to think. He hadn't killed me, and he hadn't let me see his face or hear his voice. He didn't want me to be able to identify him, which wouldn't be a concern if I never made it out alive. That left the possibility, however small, that he might let me go.

There was a scraping sound, something dragging across the floor, and then I felt my skirt being pulled up. I yelped as hands touched my waist, one on either side, and began to remove my underwear. I heard myself whimpering. Strong arms lifted me up and shoved something beneath me, some sort of bowl or bucket, and I understood. I cried, not wanting to relieve myself in front of him, not wanting to know what would happen next.

As soon as I was done, he moved the bucket, put the bag back over my head, and left. The door closed softly, and my sobs filled the room, echoing around me. He had not returned my underwear. I thought of Tom's father in the baler. I had wondered if he'd prayed to survive or die quickly. If he had prayed to survive in those first moments, he'd changed his mind later, once he realized what he was in for. It wasn't the baler that had killed him.

I didn't lack hope. Aside from the discomfort of being restrained, he hadn't gone out of his way to hurt me, and I told myself he might not want to. I moved my legs, trying to feel around for the bucket, but it was gone. Not that I could have used it as a weapon anyhow. There wasn't much I could do to fight back as long as I was tethered to a wall. I'd have to think of another way out.

# CHAPTER 21

# SARAH, NOW

The Blackburns' driveway looked like any of the dozen other dirt roads we'd passed, all of them disappearing into the woods, but a few miles after the trees closed in behind us, we faced an iron gate with an intercom. Sylvie had me press the call button and moments later the gate beeped and slid open.

It was another mile or two before we reached the Blackburns' compound in a broad clearing surrounded by towering pines. The road forked in two with a house on either side. To the right, a small white clapboard that must have been a hundred years old, and to the left, a newer two-story red cedar cabin with a pair of rocking chairs on the porch. Several other buildings were scattered around the clearing: a machine shed with a bright red International Harvester tractor parked outside, a large barn with a gambrel roof, a garage, a rustic outhouse that appeared to be for decorative purposes only. A garden bright with pumpkins and gourds basked in the sun between the houses. On the far side of the clearing, the two roads continued into the woods in different directions.

Sylvie waved me to the left. "Leave your phone in the car, if you don't mind," she said. "She doesn't like them."

Minnie leaned over the cabin's porch railing and waved as we parked and got out. "I hope you're hungry," she said. "I'm fixing a little lunch."

"Lucky us!" Sylvie said. Her enthusiasm was so over the top it sounded fake. Either she was kissing up to her soon-to-be mother-in-law, or she was a huge fan of Minnie Blackburn.

"It's so lovely to have you here, Sarabeth," Minnie said, ushering us into the cool, dim entryway and down the hall to a spacious kitchen. Everything was made of cedar—walls, floors, cabinets, countertops, a harvest table large enough to seat a dozen people. The window over the sink looked out to the woods and a gushing creek, probably the same one Sylvie could see from her and Noah's cabin.

"Thank you for offering to help out," I said.

"Oh, it's my absolute pleasure. I love to sew." She smoothed her skirt, subtly drawing attention to the perfect pleats and even stitching. "The fabric Sylvie chose is beautiful. Pale blue—Noah's favorite color."

Sylvie beamed. "Can we help you with lunch? What needs doing?"

Minnie had plates laid out on the counter, thick slices of bread on each. "Well, let's see, I have ham for sandwiches, and pimento spread, but we could use a fresh jar of pickles if you don't mind running down to the root cellar."

"Of course," Sylvie said. "Anything else?"

"Oh, I don't know, maybe a jar of peaches for dessert if you two fancy it."

"Be right back," Sylvie said.

I started to follow her out of the kitchen, but Minnie stopped me.

"Stay and visit," she said. "Your sister can manage on her own." Minnie stepped closer and placed her hand on my shoulder, and I resisted the urge to pull away. "I know you probably still think of her as the girl she was when you left. I can see it in the way you look at her. But she's a capable young woman now."

"I guess she is." Minnie's hand dropped away, though I could still feel where it had been.

"Your mother has raised her well. She'll make a fine wife, and a wonderful mother, too. You should see her with the babies at the church nursery. And she's the only one besides me who can quiet my little Rachel when she's crying."

"You . . . have a baby?" Minnie's entire existence, to my recollection, had centered on the womb—the gift of fertility, the recurrent miscarriages, her steadfast determination to trust in God's punishing, unrevealed plan.

"Yes." Her large cowlike eyes glistened. "Did Sylvie not tell you?"

"No, she didn't. She must've thought I already knew."

"It's a miracle of faith," she said. She wrapped her arms around her middle and dropped her voice to a whisper. "And I probably shouldn't say . . . it's early yet . . . but I think we might have another on the way, praise the Lord."

"Wow. Congratulations." It was hard to picture Minnie with a baby. I'd always thought of her as old, though she couldn't be much over forty. She had warned us in youth group not to wait too long to have children, that the older we grew, the less fertile we'd be. She'd had Noah when she was seventeen.

"Thank you." Minnie pulled a carving knife out of a drawer

and began to saw away at a glazed ham, thick pink slices falling away from the blade. "Sylvie'll be with me when the new baby's born," she said. "So she can help, get some firsthand experience. She wants to train as a midwife. Of course, she's eager to have a little one of her own. She's been praying."

"Yeah, that's what I've heard."

Sylvie returned with a jar in each hand and I watched her arrange pickles on a plate, spoon peaches into dainty dessert bowls. I felt like I should be helping, but I wasn't sure what to do. Minnie said grace, and while we ate, she and Sylvie chatted about the food for the wedding reception. I nodded and smiled when necessary. After we had finished and cleaned up the dishes, Minnie checked the clock.

"Sylvie, would you mind to wake Rachel from her nap and feed her while I get Sarabeth's measurements?"

"I'd be happy to," she said. She opened the freezer and took out a bag of frozen milk, like she'd done it plenty of times before.

"Let's go to my sewing room," Minnie said, leading me into the back hallway and down to the lower level. We passed a sliding glass door, and I spied a concrete hump in the backyard, the top of the root cellar sticking up out of the ground, steps descending into the earth.

There were no windows in the sewing room, but the fluorescent light overhead was painfully bright. "Here we go," she said, grabbing her measuring tape. "Hold your arms out to your sides." She reached around me to stretch the tape across my back, pulling it together over my chest, between my breasts. It felt uncomfortably intimate, and I focused on holding still, wanting to get it over with. She moved the tape to my armpit, running her fingers over my ribs, down to my waist, her hair brushing against my face.

"You know," she said, squatting to measure from my waist to

the floor, "my miracle was a long time coming. I had all but given up hope that I would ever have another child. I prayed and prayed, but it wasn't until I truly submitted myself to God's will that things changed. I realized He had a different plan for me— one I never could have imagined. My failure to bear children didn't mean I was useless. There was so much I could do to help others through my faith." She got to her feet, reaching for my arm to steady herself. "There's hope for everyone, a purpose for everyone. Even those who've lost their way."

I didn't want to listen to one of Minnie Blackburn's sermons. I eased backward, trying to put space between us, and felt the wall behind me. The urge to escape was sudden and fierce. I needed to get out of her sewing room, her basement, her house. I took a breath, reminded myself that I wasn't trapped, that I could simply leave. "I'd better get going," I said, my voice artificially cheery.

Minnie led me back upstairs, where Sylvie sat in the kitchen feeding Rachel. Minnie gently lifted the baby from Sylvie's arms. "We'll talk more tomorrow," she said to me. "I'll need you here in the evening to do your fitting."

I was relieved to finally get back in the car, where I could ground myself in familiar surroundings. I stuffed a piece of Big Red chewing gum in my mouth and focused on the taste and smell of cinnamon, the tingling sensation on my tongue—a calming sensory trick my counselor had taught me.

"Wasn't it a lovely visit?" Sylvie said. "I know I'll miss Mama, but it'll be so nice to have Minnie right down the lane."

"Yeah," I said. "How far's your cabin from here?"

"I'll show you. Just follow the road. It makes a loop through the woods."

The road dipped down into a wash alongside the creek, my

car nearly bottoming out on the rocks where spring floods had eaten away the earth. We'd gone about a mile from the main house when Sylvie's cabin appeared. It was tiny, with a peaked roof and a chimney and a stony yard sprouting patches of tickseed. Golden-green light spilled down through the trees along the creek, but the canopy above the cabin was impenetrable, cloaking it in shadow.

"It's beautiful," I said.

"Noah's been working hard to fix it up in time for the wedding. He drives all the way out here every day after his shift at the sawmill."

"Where's he living now?"

"He rents a trailer in town. He moved out a few years ago when he started his job. Minnie'd been trying to get him to move back for a while. The Blackburns have all this land out here, this great ministry they're building. They wanted him to be a part of it. After Rachel was born, he finally realized it was time to come home, settle down . . . take a wife." She adjusted her engagement ring, twisting it around her finger. "It took a lot of work and prayer, but Minnie really wanted her family all together. She can be very convincing."

I tried to picture Sylvie living in the little cabin with Noah. I remembered the way he and I used to look at each other, the shy glances, flushed skin, the electric thrill that arced through me when he touched my hand.

I turned to Sylvie. "Do you love him? Do you feel anything for him?"

"Sarabeth," she chided.

"You deserve to be in love with the person you marry."

She tilted her head, her long hair swirling in the breeze from the open windows. "Have you ever been in love?"

I hadn't. I'd never even had a real boyfriend. Noah was as close as I'd come, and I couldn't tell her that.

"It doesn't matter," she said when I didn't answer. "There's no greater love than God's. He has a plan for each of us."

Her voice was sweet and childlike, but the words sounded like something that would come out of Minnie's mouth. And no wonder, considering how Sylvie looked up to her. I'd thought at first that my sister had been brainwashed into becoming a child bride, that I just needed to get through to her, but I was starting to realize that the Sylvie I remembered wasn't real. I'd thought of her as being just like me, but in reality, she'd always been more like Mama. I didn't know whether she'd turned out this way because it was her nature all along or because of how Mama raised her. It was impossible to separate the two, and it didn't matter. The result was the same. This was who she was. It wasn't something I could talk her out of.

"I just want the best for you, Syl."

She squeezed my arm. "That's what I want for you, too. Now let's get home. There's so much to do."

We continued through the woods, passing a metal livestock barn and a trailer set back in the trees. I could make out a figure at the edge of the barn, watching us go by. I remembered what Tom had said about Ronnie living on the property.

"Is that Ronnie Darling?"

"Yes," she said. "He works here."

"I always thought he was kind of creepy," I said.

"You shouldn't judge him. It's amazing how he's turned his life around. Such a testament to the Blackburns' ministry."

"So he's changed?"

"We're all imperfect, Sarabeth. When you invest in the soul, it pays dividends."

I mostly tuned out Sylvie's chatter on the way home. Once we got back to an area that had cell service, my phone beeped with notifications. I waited until we reached our driveway to check them, Sylvie watching me. Helen had texted a picture of Gypsy gnawing on an enormous bone from the butcher. Farrow's message was two words long: "Call me."

"Can I let you out here so I can make a call?" I asked Sylvie. "I don't have service down at the house."

"I'll wait with you."

"It's sort of . . . private. If you don't mind."

She cocked her head to the side. "Who are you calling?"

"It's just something for work."

"All right. Don't be long."

I waited for the door to shut behind her and then dialed Farrow.

"Hey," he said. "Couple things." He sounded wired, like he'd been chugging coffee all day. "Update on the testing. Most of the blood samples matched you and only you. But the one that came back inconclusive last time . . . they wouldn't say on the record since they're not finished, but I think they found someone else's blood mixed with yours. Hopefully there's enough material to extract at least a partial profile."

"That's great! Where does that get us?"

"Well, if there's enough information, they can check for a match in the system. If there's no match, we can try the genealogical databases, see if we can get some help with that, narrow it down. There's been some success with that route, but it could take a while, unfortunately."

"Can't they speed things up?"

"They're doing what they can. If we can come up with a suspect to test against, that would help." He cleared his throat. "The other thing I wanted to tell you—I followed up on the Winter Meeting. The person who chaired the social committee last year lives in Bellwood. What is that, maybe ten miles from Wisteria?"

"Yeah. It's one of those wide spots in the road that used to be a town."

"Do you happen to know a Carlene Ford?"

"Carlene doesn't sound familiar. But I know the last name. There're lots of Fords around here. I can ask a friend of mine; she's probably related somehow."

"I'm thinking Carlene's husband might be the one to look at. Leon Ford. He was picked up on suspicion of committing a lewd act with a minor a couple years back, but no charges were filed."

"Shit," I said. "That's Retta's brother."

"You know him?"

"Yeah. Sort of. He goes to my family's church."

"The same church Eva Winters belongs to?"

"Yes. Holy Rock. And Leon . . . he did something else, a long time ago. There wouldn't be any record of it."

"What?"

"He did something to Retta, when they were younger. He'd go into her room at night. I don't know the details. Her family kept it quiet, like it never happened."

"Okay," he said. "I'm going to take a closer look at him, see what I can find out about his movements, if he could have been in the right places at the right times. And I'd like to talk to your friend, if you think she'd be willing."

"I don't know," I said. "I doubt she'd talk to a stranger about it, but I'll see if she'll talk to me."

After we hung up, I sat in the car looking out at the farm stand, the cornfield. I didn't know Leon well, but I'd seen him in church every week. He knew who I was, that I was Retta's friend.

I tried to remember how the man in the mask had looked walking toward me, the shape of his shoulders, the heft of his body as he crushed me to his chest among the cornstalks. I couldn't have said if it was Leon, if it was his blood that had mixed with mine on the slip. But maybe Retta would know.

# CHAPTER 22

# SARABETH, THEN

## AGE 17

I drifted in and out, my head heavy and my mind fuzzed with static, unable to track how much time passed before I was able to think somewhat clearly. I wondered if he had put something in my water, and why he would bother, since I couldn't get away. My stomach twisted with hunger or nausea and I thought of the Olive Garden in Branson, where the popular kids from Wisteria went to dinner before prom. Tom had eaten there once with his grandparents on the way back from picking out his father's gravestone. He said it was the nicest restaurant he'd ever been to aside from Red Lobster, and I had desperately wanted to go there. It was a stupid, stupid dream to have. Italian food wasn't even my favorite. But I wanted to go to a fancy sit-down restaurant in a strapless prom dress and order a Coke with unlimited refills. I had never gotten to go to Olive Garden, or Red Lobster, and now I never would.

Mama would have been ashamed if she knew I was thinking about such trivial things instead of praying. She had tired herself out trying to mold me into an obedient, God-fearing girl, one who wore a pleasant expression and behaved selflessly and worked hard without complaint. It did not come naturally to me, but I learned how to fake it to avoid her biting criticism, her sharp pinches, the extra chores, and occasional whippings. I hated how it felt, smiling when I didn't want to, swallowing the words I couldn't say. It became second nature, and I hated that, too, but even when the behavior was automatic, it wasn't authentic. Underneath, I remained unchanged. It had all been a waste of my mother's time, a waste of my life. The man in the mask had made a mistake if he'd sought a girl like the one I pretended to be. The long hair and frumpy dress were merely a costume. But if he thought I was soft and submissive, maybe I could convince him that I wasn't a threat, that I would behave if he'd untie me.

I sang quietly to myself as I waited, a song from the Taylor Swift *Red* CD that Tom used to play on repeat. He knew all the words, but I could only remember the chorus, so I sang it over and over. Taylor said everything would be all right. It was close enough to a prayer.

Finally, the door made a gentle swooshing sound as it swept open and closed, and the man was in the room with me again.

"Hello?" I said, my voice shaky. "My name's Sarabeth." There was no response. "Thank you for the food and water," I continued, trying to infuse each word with meekness and gratitude.

He moved closer and I flinched as he grasped the restraint at my wrist. For one breathless moment, I thought he meant to unfasten it, but he only tugged to make sure it was secure. He knelt down between my legs, his weight on the bar that both bound them together and kept them apart.

"Please," I said, the word squeaking out of my mouth. "Please."

His hand met my throat, warm fingers sliding inside the collar of my dress and pulling it taut, and I heard the unmistakable sound of scissors, the bright chirp of the blades as they bit down on each mouthful of fabric, moving from my neck to my chest to my stomach to my lap. He sliced the dress all the way through the hem, leaving the slip beneath intact, and moved on to the sleeves, the dull side of the blade gliding along the flesh of my arms until the fabric dropped free, one side and then the other.

The scissors clattered to the floor, and with both hands he eased the slip up to my waist, and then, after a pause, wrenched it up to my armpits and flung the fabric over my face. He unclasped my bra without touching my breasts. There was a slight softening of the darkness, and I knew, despite the blindfold, that he'd turned on a small light. I imagined him looking at me, exposed like a specimen on display.

"Please don't," I said. My voice was muffled, and he gave no indication that he heard me. Goosebumps popped, tiny hairs rose up. I tried to brace myself for unknown horrors, to distance myself from my own body, but his touch, when it came, was cursory, clinical. Almost like an exam. It made me think of Mr. Darling with the livestock, inspecting a cow. Something cold and wet brushed my skin and I squirmed. It was a washrag. He swiped it back and forth across my body, neck, armpit, downward. I heard it being rinsed and wrung out as he went.

Finally he withdrew his hands and I couldn't tell whether he was done or just pausing before whatever would come next. I shivered as the air chilled my damp skin. The dread intensified with each heartbeat, building toward a crescendo that wouldn't come. I wanted to scream at him to get it over with, because whatever it was, it would bring an end to the unbearable agony of waiting.

A minute passed and I heard him breathing, making small,

soft noises in his throat. Finally I heard him pick up the scissors and my entire body tensed, my teeth grinding together as I imagined the gleaming blades inching closer. Cold metal kissed my breastbone, traced down my rib cage, and then the slip was pulled back into place, the pressure removed from my ankles as he stood and backed away. I tried to drag my legs beneath my slip like a snail shrinking into its shell. The door closed and he was gone, and I was alone again in the dark.

# CHAPTER 23

# SARAH, NOW

On Thursday, Sylvie and I were busy making sheet cake and cupcakes and frosting. She didn't want her wedding cake to be fancy, but she had been practicing piping simple flower decorations with the buttercream. The boys worked on tidying the shady side of the yard for the reception and then went to help Daddy haul folding tables and chairs over from the church. I didn't get a chance to slip away and call Retta until after dinner, when Sylvie shooed me out of the kitchen.

"Minnie'll be expecting you for your fitting," she said. "I can't wait to see how the dress looks."

"You're not coming with me?"

"I need to frost the cupcakes," she said. "And do a hundred other things." She swooped in and kissed my cheek. "Say hello to Minnie for me."

I called Retta when I reached the top of the driveway. There was a chorus of wailing in the background when she answered.

"Is it not a good time?" I said.

"No, it's fine. They didn't nap this afternoon, so they're getting cranky." One of the boys' cries escalated into a piercing scream.

"I'll try to be quick," I said. "You know how we were talking about what happened to me . . . how I want to find out who did it. I wanted to ask you about something. About Leon."

"Oh."

"I know you don't like to talk about it, but . . . I thought maybe, if there were similarities . . ."

"You think it was my brother?"

"He's shown that he's capable of something like that." I heard a door shut on Retta's end of the line, muting the boys' cries.

"It's completely different," she hissed. "That was so long ago, Sarabeth. We were kids. It's over and done with. He was married, with a family, when you disappeared. He's got five children now, including three little girls of his own. He never did anything like that again."

"Yes, he did," I said. "Not that long ago. No charges were filed, but he was suspected of committing lewd acts with a minor."

"What does that even mean? How would you know something like that?"

"I'm just trying to figure this out. So it doesn't happen to anyone else. What you told me about Eva Winters . . . you said your nieces loved her. Leon's girls?"

"She watched the girls at church! Maybe sat for them a couple of times at the house."

"It could be more than a coincidence. There are other girls, Retta, who are missing. You could help."

"You sound crazy," she said. "I don't know anything about any of this. And I'm not going to help you drag my family into it.

I'm sorry for what happened to you, I truly am, but sometimes it's best to let things go and move on."

"Is that what you did? You buried it all and now you're fine? You never worry about your little nieces?"

"Leon would *never*," she said, her breath whistling angrily through the phone. "Is this why you came to see me? Is this the whole reason you're here?"

"Of course not!" I said. "I came for Sylvie. And I came to see you because I missed my best friend. I didn't mean to upset you."

"Well, you did. And you're wrong. My brother's got nothing to do with this. And I've got nothing else to say to you." The line went silent, and when I called back, she didn't pick up.

When I arrived at the Blackburns' place, Minnie led me directly to the basement and the windowless sewing room. "Go on and take off your dress so we can try this on and see if I need to make any adjustments."

I waited for her to leave the room, but she didn't, so I turned my back to her, unbuttoned my sundress, and stepped out of it. She made a disdainful clucking noise, no doubt appalled by my lack of a slip, and helped me into the maid of honor dress. It draped oppressively over my body, covering every bit of flesh but my hands and head. She tugged at the powder blue fabric, pinned the hem. She pulled the collar tight around my neck and then stood back to assess me, her tiny mouth puckered up.

"Lovely," she said. "It softens you."

"Can I take it off now?"

"Let me help," she said. "Don't want to stick you with a pin." She lifted the dress up over my head, and for a moment too long I was trapped in the voluminous fabric, arms caught, face covered. Panic fluttered through me, and I thrashed like I was drowning. "Hold still," she said, pulling it free. "I've got it."

I measured my breaths, trying to calm myself, but I still felt the grip of anxiety like a hand on my throat, even after I was back in my own clothes and on my way upstairs. The kitchen was growing dim in the fading light.

"Why don't you sit down and I'll get you a slice of banana bread," Minnie said. "The pastor will be home in a little while. I know he'd love the chance to catch up with you."

In the curio cabinet behind her, a dozen Precious Moments figurines stared out through the glass, all white as ghosts, eyes like black teardrops. "That's so kind of you, but I need to help Sylvie with the cake. She's expecting me."

"We've barely had a chance to talk," she said. "And we're about to be family. Stay for a glass of tea, at least."

She didn't wait for an answer before fetching the nearly empty pitcher. What was left in the bottom looked dark as tar. She took an old-fashioned metal ice tray out of the freezer and whacked it on the counter to loosen the cubes. Amid the cracking ice, I heard something else. Footsteps coming down the hall. I'd hoped to get out before Pastor Rick showed up. It wasn't the pastor, though, who appeared in the doorway. I froze.

"Noah," Minnie said. "I didn't know you were coming by."

He stared at me, his neck reddening below the beard that covered much of his face. I wasn't sure why I'd ever thought he resembled Albert Ingalls. He looked nothing like Albert aside from his suspenders and the dark mop of hair. He was more of an Isaiah Edwards, burly and moonfaced, his blue eyes brooding. Then his lips parted, and for a moment I was back in the church basement, desperately trying to decipher whatever wordless message he might be trying to send me. I forced myself to look away. That was the distant past. Noah was no longer a boy I had a crush on. He was a grown man about to marry a sixteen-year-old girl—my little sister—and as much as I hated that for Sylvie, I had no desire to trade places with her.

"Where are your manners, son?" Minnie said.

He nodded at me. "Hello, Sarabeth."

I nodded back.

"We were just about to sit down and have some tea. Your father should be home soon. You could join us, if you'd like."

"No thank you," he said. He sounded agitated, almost angry, and my stomach twisted. "I stopped by to talk to you about something."

Minnie pursed her lips, the ice tray dangling from her hand. "Surely it can wait."

"It's all right," I said, grateful for an excuse to escape. "I need to get going anyway. Thank you again. It was . . . nice to see you, Noah."

Minnie hurried after me and caught me at the door. "You'll have to come back tomorrow night to pick up the dress," she said. "I'll have it all pressed and you can try it on one last time to make sure it's just right."

It was nearly dark as I walked to my car. Across the garden, I saw what looked like a scarecrow in front of the old farmhouse, dressed in a flannel shirt and straw hat. As I opened my door, I heard a whistle and turned around. The scarecrow had moved closer, almost to the edge of the garden. I jumped as its arm rose up and a familiar voice called my name.

"Sarabeth. Hey." I kept my hand on the car door, bracing myself as Ronnie Darling jogged over to me.

"I thought it was you," he said. He took off the straw hat and raked his hand through his hair. "Saw you drive by with Sylvie the other day."

"Yeah," I said. "It's me."

"Been a while," he said. The corner of his mouth turned up in a coy smile, but he maintained eye contact, not dropping his gaze to scan my body like he used to do. "How've you been?"

"Good. How about you? I heard you're working for the Blackburns now."

"Yes, ma'am." He nodded soberly. "Helping out with the ministry. Finally found my calling."

"That's great," I said. "What do you do, exactly? Tom said you're selling dogs."

He chuckled. "That's part of it, yeah."

"Why dogs, though? How does that fit with the ministry?"

"Money," he said matter-of-factly. "To keep the whole operation running. Pastors don't make much, and donations only go so far. Gotta come from somewhere."

It felt strange to be having a normal conversation with him. I remembered what Tom had said, that Ronnie was putting on an act, that he didn't buy his transformation. It was too soon to tell, but there was definitely something different about him. Maybe it was partly because the dynamics had changed. I was no longer at his mercy, enduring his taunts and innuendos. I didn't have to suffer quietly if he tried to intimidate me. I could say something. I could leave. I was wary of him, but that only made me more curious about what he was up to. If Sylvie was going to be joining the Blackburn family, I wanted to know what kind of business they were running.

"I love dogs," I said. "I've been thinking of getting one. Could I see them?"

"We don't usually take people back to the kennels."

"It's just me," I said sweetly. "Us."

His eyes narrowed as he gauged whether I was flirting or not. If he'd changed, he hadn't changed that much. I looked up at him, wide-eyed and expectant.

"All right," he said. "Just for you."

"Get in," I said. "I'll give you a ride."

"Yes, ma'am," he said, drawing out the words. He bit his lip and I wondered if it was killing him not to make a dirty joke. I knew how hard it was to keep up the appearance of being something you're not.

I could feel him watching me while I drove. "So what else do you do here?" I asked. "You said the dogs are just one part of it."

"Lots of things. Take care of the property, handle the guest-house."

"Guesthouse?"

"The old farmhouse." He gestured behind us. "That was their house up until a few years ago, when they built the new one. Now it's part of the ministry. People stay there sometimes, folks the Blackburns are helping out."

"So . . . the dog money paid for their new house?"

"I guess. But anyway, the main thing I do is the websites. Separate ones for Holy Rock, the ministry, the dogs. Go on and pull up by the trailer," he said.

I parked next to his pickup and we got out. The air had cooled off since dark set in, and my arms and legs prickled with goose-bumps. There were no lights on in his trailer, or outside the buildings. Ventilation fans hummed, blowing air in and out of the kennel. They weren't loud enough to drown out the barking.

"What kind of dog you thinking of?" Ronnie asked. "We got some coonhounds we mostly sell to people around here for hunting—blueticks, walkers, redbones—but we make more money off the little prissy ones. Ship 'em all over." He pulled a key ring from his pocket and unlocked the door. The dogs yipped and whined. When he flicked on the light, it revealed rows of stacked wire cages, dogs of all sizes squirming inside. I was used to animal smells from working at the shelter, but even with the fans going, the stench was overpowering.

"There's so many," I said. "More than I thought."

He seemed to take it as a compliment. "Business is growing. Trying to keep up." He stripped off his flannel shirt, revealing a thin T-shirt underneath. He had a new tattoo since I'd seen him last, a thorn-wrapped cross on his forearm. The dogs whimpered and writhed and cried, rattling their cages, and I wanted to cover my ears.

"How much for a little one?" I said.

"You can get a cripple for cheap—bad leg, whatnot. Healthy ones go for a grand, maybe more. Depends which breed."

"Guess I'll have to save up."

"Let me know if you're interested," he said, moving closer. "Maybe we can work out a deal."

I didn't flinch. I clenched my jaw and tried to smile just right, not too much, not too little. "You'd do that for me?"

"I might."

He was close enough that I could feel the heat from his body. I wanted to bolt for the door. "I better get home for now," I said. "But I'll be back."

"You know where to find me," he said.

My hands were shaking when I got in the car. I dug out the card Melissa had given me, the one for the animal rescue group. When I reached the gate, I texted the tip line and dropped a location pin, hoping it would go through. *Gated property, road forks to the right, livestock barn full of caged dogs.* If animal control showed up, the Blackburns would know it was me who'd turned them in, but I didn't care. They deserved to be shut down. I wondered if Sylvie had been inside the kennel, if she thought the abuse was justified to support the ministry. She always had a soft heart for animals when she was little. Maybe that had changed. I couldn't be sure anymore.

I pulled up my notifications. There were seven missed calls, all from Farrow, and one voicemail. I pressed play. As usual, all he said was "Call me back," but I could tell from his voice that I didn't want to hear what he had to say.

# CHAPTER 24

# SARABETH, THEN

## AGE 18

My head buzzed, like my brain had been scoured with sandpaper. I couldn't begin to guess the day. Time had stretched like taffy, folding over itself, melting back together. He was in the room again, but something was different. A sense of urgency. He did the bucket routine first, with less patience than before, and I began to worry that whatever was going to happen would happen soon. I was weak and desperately thirsty, but I knew if he knocked me out again, any hope of fighting back would be gone. He removed the bag from my head and pressed the bottle to my cracked lips, and I twisted away. He grabbed my jaw to force me to drink and I let out a jagged scream, using all my strength to thrash my body. It startled him and he jumped back. The bucket rattled and the bottle dropped to the floor, and I felt something soaking into the blanket beneath me, wetting my slip—water or urine or both.

He made a grating sound in his throat and the blanket was wrenched out from under me. Cold metal touched my wrist and I heard a click. A searing pain blazed through my arms and down my back as he released me from the wall and cuffed my hands together in front of me.

He yanked me to my feet and I stumbled and fell, my ankles still shackled and my legs weak and unaccustomed to standing. He got me upright again, more carefully this time, and half dragged, half carried me through the doorway. I tried to scream again, but my throat was raw and all that came out was a strangled wheeze.

He secured the handcuffs to something just above my head, and then I heard water running, splashing, gurgling down a drain. A bathtub, or a shower. There was a metallic scrape, the sound of scissors opening, and he grabbed the back of my slip, pulling the fabric taut like he had done when he cut me out of my dress. As the blades closed together, they caught in my hair and he sliced right through. I could feel a section come loose. That seemed to anger him and he started chopping, the soft weight of my hair falling away in hunks. I thought of how Mama would line the three boys up outside for haircuts. My little brothers would worry because Grams had told them if a bird uses your hair to make a nest, you'll get a headache.

Tears tracked down my cheeks. I didn't care if he cut off all my hair. It was heavy and hot and I wouldn't miss it, but I had dreamed of going to Cathy's Corner Cuts in town like a normal girl, putting on a plastic cape, sitting in front of the lighted mirror, Cathy freeing me from my hair, releasing me like an animal from a trap. It was one more reminder of the life I wanted and couldn't have, the life that had been stolen from me because my father lusted over a truck-stop waitress and my mother couldn't bear it. I'd been waiting for years to turn eighteen and reclaim my life, and I hadn't come so close just to die in this basement.

He was right behind me, holding on to my hair, and I did the only thing I could think of. I gritted my teeth and whipped my head back, my skull cracking against bone, and he gasped. He clutched at me and we fell together, the force of it ripping down the bar I'd been tethered to. The scissors clattered to the floor. Bright stars of pain strobed in my head and I clawed at my blindfold as I rolled off him, but it was taped too tightly and there wasn't time. I scrambled for the scissors before he could get up, knowing it could be my last chance. I swept my hands over the floor, and there they were. I looped my fingers through the handles, and as he tried to snatch them away from me, I held tight, blades closed, and stabbed blindly. He let out a guttural wail and I stabbed him again and again until his fist rocketed into my face.

# CHAPTER 25

# SARAH, NOW

I was back on the road when I got through to Farrow.

"Where are you?" he said.

"Driving."

"So am I. Heading your way, actually. Do you think you could meet me at the Shell station in Lead Hill? I need to talk to you in person."

"Oh," I said. "I guess so. It'll take me at least twenty minutes to get there."

"That's fine," he said. "I'll be waiting."

He hung up before I could ask him any questions, and I spent the drive searching for radio stations amid the static, trying to keep myself from cataloging all the different kinds of bad news he might bring. When I arrived, I found him in the dark parking lot, leaning against the Tahoe. It was covered in dust, as though he'd taken the back roads.

"Sarah," he said. "I'm sorry."

"What happened? Did the blood tests come back?"

"No. They found Destiny," he said. "Or at least they think so.

Her remains. They haven't been able to get a positive identification."

"What?" An icy numbness spread across my chest, down my arms to my fingertips. I'd known all along it was a possibility, that we wouldn't find her in time, but I didn't want to believe it. "Where did they find . . . was it the same place? The rest stop?"

"No." He exhaled heavily, his breath shushing out through his lips. "No. At the farm. She was never taken. She never left home."

"At the farm? But . . . the cadaver dogs were there. They searched everywhere. The sheds, the fields, the woods. They would've found her."

"The dogs didn't find anything because she . . . her remains were so badly burned. There was barely anything left—bones, teeth, nearly everything was broken down. They can't even ID her because there's nothing to test, that's why it hasn't been confirmed—burned too long and too hot for DNA. They found a bit of molar, a few larger pieces of bone. All they can say for sure is the remains belong to a human female, likely someone in her teens."

An old pickup pulled into the lot, jolting over potholes, its headlights briefly blinding me before they shut off.

"How was she found, then? If there was nothing left?"

"Trina went to a clinic the next town over to see about a skin infection. Remember how she was wearing long sleeves in the heat? Her arm was blistered up. Told the nurse she got burned using gasoline to get that big signal fire going for Destiny. While she was there, she tried to get a refill on her Ambien, but she'd just gotten it filled back home, the week before. Nurse thought something was off and called in a tip, and the sheriff decided to go back and sift through the ashes. They found a metal button from a pair of jeans. Called in forensics."

"But . . . Trina—what did she say?"

"Not much. She hasn't confessed to anything. Vance had deleted texts on his phone from Destiny's number. Doesn't appear to be anything inappropriate, but my guess is Trina found out. Maybe she worried her daughter was getting to be competition for her boyfriend, or maybe she was just pissed that Destiny disobeyed her—that she was hiding a phone, texting boys without permission. You remember what Destiny's friend said, what happened last time Trina got mad, threw her phone in the pond. I don't know. Sheriff didn't find any Ambien at the house. They're speculating Trina drugged her at dinner and put her in the firepit that night. The sleeping pills wouldn't have been enough to kill her." Farrow looked away, his face lost in shadow. "So she was likely still alive when the fire started."

"Oh, god. Trina said it was a signal fire. To light her way home. The prayer vigil—"

"Yeah. She kept that fire going for days. Destiny was there all along, right in front of us. People singing and praying while her bones burned down to ash." He cleared his throat. "For now, they can't prove it's Destiny, but they have the circumstantial evidence that could implicate Trina or Vance or maybe both of them. I don't know."

"I can't stop thinking of that camper. It was awful, but it was her room, and she had her poster, and her stuffed animals. She was looking forward to making a new dress for the dance. She just wanted a phone to text her friends, like a normal kid."

"I know," he said. "I know. I'm sorry, Sarah. I never should have gotten you involved. I pushed you into it for selfish reasons, and I shouldn't have. It was a mistake. The whole thing was a mistake."

"No," I said. "I wanted to help. I still do. Abby's still out there."

"I don't know," he said. "I was wrong. About the connections. I was looking for things that weren't there, ignoring what I didn't want to see." He was silent for a moment. "I haven't been completely honest with you, but I need you to understand why I did what I did."

"What do you mean?"

"It's . . . I'm not on Abby's case. There is no case, not officially."

"I don't get it. She's not missing?" I remembered googling missing girls with her name, not finding her.

"No, she is, but . . . I never had the authority to drag you into this," he said. "My motivations were personal, and I should have told you, right from the start."

"What motivations? Just tell me what's going on."

"You remember the story I told you, at the cabin? About when I was a kid. About my baby sister."

"Yes."

"I didn't tell you her name," he said.

For a moment I wasn't certain that he meant what I thought he meant, that despite the look on his face, I might have misunderstood. I had to say it out loud to be sure. "It's Abby."

"Yes."

I thought back to what he'd said at the river, wondered how I'd missed it. He'd wanted to find her and apologize to her. He blamed himself for not taking better care of her, for their family splitting up.

"When I found her adoptive parents, they didn't want me to see her. It took a while for me to figure out she wasn't there. They hadn't reported her missing. When I finally got them to talk to me, they said they figured she'd run away, but I didn't believe it. I was sure something had happened to her."

"Why didn't you just tell me?"

"Would you have talked to me if I showed up at your house, some random guy asking for your help to find his long-lost sister? I needed you to trust me, believe me. The badge, the case—that gave me the credibility I needed. After we met, I wanted to tell you, but you were skittish. You didn't want to get involved as it was. I really did think your case had some connection to Abby. I believed it. I needed to. Because you were let go. I wanted Abby to come back, too. I wanted to believe that I could find her alive." He looked down at the pavement, at the weeds growing through the cracks.

"Maybe you will."

"Yeah," he said. "I hope so. I meant what I said about helping with your case, too. But they have nothing to do with each other. There's no need for you to be involved. This was a dead end."

"How can you be so sure? What about the new leads? Leon? Everett Linley? I talked to Retta, and she said Eva Winters baby-sat Leon's kids."

"Everett got drunk and crashed his truck into a Piggly Wiggly store, striking and injuring a cashier. Nothing close to kidnapping. Suffered a brain injury in the accident, which he's still recovering from. We don't have any evidence that Leon did anything to anyone. No charges were ever filed against him. I'll track down the Winters girl, make sure she's where they say she is, see if she's okay. If she's not . . . if there's any evidence of a crime, it'll be investigated. But right now any similarities be-tween your case and Abby's are purely coincidental. The church, the homeschooling—how many families around here have that in common? Too many to count. Destiny had that, too, and it didn't mean anything. I'm right back where I started, and I'm wondering if maybe instead of chasing leads I should be search-ing Abby's parents' house, digging up their backyard."

I wanted to comfort him somehow, but I didn't know what to say. Maybe he was right.

He shoved his hands in his pockets and looked me in the eye. "What you did . . . what you went through to help me . . . I don't think I really appreciated how hard that was for you. I'm so sorry about all of this, the position I put you in, the pressure. Mislead-ing you. It wasn't fair and it wasn't right. And I understand if you're angry. If you never want to see my face again. But if you ever need me—if you need anything, or nothing—just call me, and I'm there."

He watched me get back in my car, and I gripped the steering wheel until I could no longer feel my hands. I sat there and cried after Farrow pulled away. I was angry that he'd manipulated me, that he hadn't felt like he could tell me the truth from the beginning, but I understood why he'd done it. If my sister were missing—if it was Sylvie—I would do anything. I didn't regret getting involved. On our trip to Lone Ridge, I'd begun to think that maybe I could actually do something to help other girls like me. I had felt, however briefly, that I wasn't powerless. But Des-tiny was dead and maybe Abby was, too, and I was busy making crafts and baking cupcakes for my sister's wedding, a wedding I had naïvely thought I might be able to stop.

I'd been wrong about so many things, including Sylvie. She didn't want me to rescue her. She was going to marry Noah

Blackburn, and I couldn't convince her otherwise. She wasn't like me. She was content with the choices she'd made. There was nothing she wanted to change. I'd been given a second chance at life, something Destiny would never have, and I spent it in fear, afraid to let people know me, holding myself back from the things I truly wanted. I was barely even living.

# CHAPTER 26

# SARABETH, THEN

## AGE 18

I came to in a moving vehicle, a tarp covering me. I'd been hog-tied, my wrists and ankles bound together so I could barely move. Everything swirled when I tried to turn my head, and a wave of nausea rolled over me. I smelled blood. I could feel it beginning to dry on my face, down my chest. My slip was cold and wet, my hands sticky. I wasn't dead but maybe he thought I was, and he was going to dump my body. That might be the only option I had left, to lie still, pretend to be lifeless.

The vehicle slowed and vibrated as it rolled onto gravel, and then it came to a stop. I tried to keep my breathing quiet, shallow, and when the door opened I stopped breathing altogether. I stayed limp, but as he dragged me out, my hip caught jagged metal and my skin tore. A sound escaped my mouth and he paused and I feared it was the end.

He laid me down on my side, weeds and gravel scraping my bare skin, and crouched over me, his hair brushing against my face as he leaned close. I didn't flinch. I imagined him watching my chest, listening for my breath. I repeated one word over and over in my head. It wasn't a prayer. I was begging. *Please please please please please.*

He got up. I heard his shoes crunching and a door slammed and he was peeling away and then he was gone.

My body shuddered in relief. I gulped cool air. When my breathing slowed, I listened, and heard traffic nearby. The rumble of semis. I had to be close to a highway.

I struggled against my restraints but couldn't work them loose, so I painfully contorted myself until I could claw at my blindfold with my fingernails. The duct tape had been tightly wrapped around and around, melded to my hair and skin, but I managed to peel it up enough to see the sky. It was nighttime. There was pink light on the horizon, though I didn't know whether it was east or west, if the sun was rising or setting.

I couldn't see much through the weeds, so I listened to the traffic to figure out which way to go. I needed to get to the road where I could be found. I couldn't get up, but I could scoot and roll, and that's what I did until I saw headlights.

I dragged myself onto the shoulder of the highway, hoping someone would notice me. Cars passed by and I wondered what I must look like in the dark. Wreckage from an accident. A wounded animal.

Finally, as the pink light began to turn yellow and spread up into the sky, a car sped by and then screeched onto the shoulder twenty yards down the road and began to back up. A woman got out and ran toward me. She had silver hair and wore an old-fashioned brooch on her jacket like my grandma used to do. She gaped at me, horrified, shrugged off her jacket, and draped it over me. She waited with me for the ambulance and held my hand. It was covered in blood. Mine. Hopefully his.

A Missouri state highway patrolman in a big hat asked me questions while the paramedics examined me.

"What's your name?"

"Sarabeth Shepherd." My voice creaked like an old screen door.

"And where are you from?"

"Wisteria. I was kidnapped."

"When was that? Last night?"

"September twenty-fifth."

The patrolman exchanged glances with one of the paramedics. "You're sure about that?"

"Yes. It was almost my birthday."

"That was over a week ago."

"A week?"

"Was that Wisteria, you said? Arkansas?"

"Yes." It wasn't often that anyone disappeared from Wisteria. I figured law enforcement would be on the lookout.

"Huh," he said. "There's nobody been reported missing from Wisteria. Or anywhere else around those parts."

His words floated through my head like bits of dust, slowly drifting down and finally settling. It didn't make sense. Maybe it was a mistake. Maybe he'd missed it somehow, being across the state line in Missouri. I wanted to tell him that my family was looking for me, that they'd miss me if I'd been gone for an entire week. But now I wasn't sure that was true. From the look on his face, I wasn't sure he'd believe me anyway.

# CHAPTER 27

# SARAH, NOW

Friday morning I was still reeling. I'd barely slept, thinking about Destiny and what her mother had done to her. I'd begun to believe Farrow's theory that she and Abby and I were linked, that finding Destiny would lead us to Abby and uncover the truth of what had happened to me. I hadn't wanted to dig into my own past until Farrow had convinced me that it might help someone else. But we never had a chance to save Destiny, and we were no closer to finding Abby than we had been at the beginning.

The more I thought about it, though, the less I was convinced that Farrow had been wrong about everything. Maybe the person who'd taken me hadn't hurt anyone else, but what if he had? What if he was targeting girls like me? Like Retta. And Eva Winters. Girls hidden away in the hills and hollers, the only record of their existence a name scrawled inside the cover of a family Bible. Girls who wouldn't tell or wouldn't be believed. I couldn't shake Leon from my head, but Retta, who knew him best, was no longer speaking to me.

I was able to distract myself for a while by helping Luke and Paul in the fields, harvesting pumpkins and gourds and cornstalks to use as decorations for Sylvie's reception. I was surprised to find myself actually enjoying it. I'd never thought I'd miss farmwork, but I liked the smell of the earth, being outdoors, testing my strength. It felt different, too, now that no one was standing over me. I was here by choice.

For a long time, when I thought of home, everything snarled together in one ugly knot, but now that I was here, it was easier to tease apart the tangled threads. I had never hated the farm, the sweeping beauty of the land. What I had hated was the loss of myself, the act I was forced to put on, the suffocating dresses and submissive smile. I had loved sitting alone in the sunlight, watching the cloud shadows move over the distant hills, listening to the wind sift through the trees. Those were the things that had grounded me. In the field, I could breathe deeply without counting my breaths.

The sky grew overcast, the air humid and stagnant. The boys worked quietly. There was no conversation, no joking around, and I wondered if they were like that all the time, or only because I was here. When we had what we needed, we hauled everything back to the house and got washed up for supper. I wasn't hungry and didn't feel like sitting through another big family meal listening to everyone talk around me, so I decided to skip out and go into town to buy Sylvie a wedding present. I left a note in case anyone noticed my chair was empty.

It was after five when I got to town, so the stoplights had switched to flashing red. I'd forgotten about it being Friday night, and the main strip was clogged with teenagers cruising in a loop between Dairy Queen at one end and the Farm & Home at the other.

As I passed the storefronts, most already dark, I realized my options would be extremely limited. Not that I even knew what I was looking for. I had no idea what Sylvie wanted or needed for her little cabin and hadn't been thoughtful enough to ask. I'd been too busy hoping that the wedding wouldn't happen. I made the loop twice before turning on Third Street and heading toward our old house.

I'd worried that it wouldn't look the same, but the changes were subtle. It looked nicer than when we lived there. The dingy white siding had been painted yellow, the unwieldy evergreen shrubs lining the front ripped out and replaced with a bed of smooth river rocks. There was a basketball goal in the driveway and a big green "W" painted on the concrete to let everyone know that a Wisteria High Wildcat lived there. The light was on in my bedroom window upstairs. I kept driving, creeping past Jack's house. The crabapple tree was still there, a pink trike sitting in the grass beneath it. I stopped when I came to Mulberry Drive. If I followed it to the edge of town, I'd be at Retta's parents' house. I sat at the intersection, no cars coming or going in either direction, trying to decide what to do.

After a minute or two, I turned back toward Main and pulled into the Price Chopper parking lot. There was a fall display out front, with potted mums and bales of hay and garden tools. I grabbed a crimson mum and a hand shovel and went inside to find a card. The selection was limited, so I picked a random congratulations card, not realizing until I got in the checkout line that the message was more suited to a graduation or promotion than a wedding. *Congratulations! All your hard work has paid off!* It would be more fitting for Mama, who'd probably worked harder than anyone to marry her daughter to the pastor's son.

As the clerk scanned my items, I looked up and saw a familiar figure walking by. It was Jack. His hair was thinning, though he still wore it long in front and swept to the side like he had back in school. The name tag on his polo shirt read ASSISTANT MANAGER. He nodded curtly in my direction as he passed, his mouth pressed into a flat, closemouthed smile, the sort of polite acknowledgment a manager might give any customer in his store. I couldn't tell if he was pretending not to know who I was or truly didn't recognize me. On my way out, I was tempted to do something spiteful, arrange the produce in vulgar anatomical vignettes, the way Everett and his other friends used to do at the farm stand in an attempt to get a reaction from me. I settled for bumping into a tower of oranges and hearing them thump to the floor, one after another, hoping Jack would have to pick them up. There wasn't time for anything else. I had something more important to do.

I had to be sure about Leon. I couldn't let it go. If Retta wouldn't talk to me, I would dig up her secrets myself, pull them out of the earth where they'd been festering and expose them to the light.

I drove past Retta's parents' house at the northern edge of town and parked behind the abandoned general store that had been slowly rotting into the ground since we were kids. I crept through the dark field that backed the house, carrying the hand shovel I'd bought at Price Chopper. When I got close enough that someone might have spied me from a rear window, I dropped to my knees and crawled through the weeds.

I knew approximately where Retta had buried the jars, just outside the fence at the edge of the backyard, behind her mother's flower garden. Heady clouds of sweet autumn clematis climbed the wire fence, their white blossoms glowing in the moonlight and shielding me from view. I leaned all my weight on the shovel, trying to push the blade into the earth, but the hard-packed clay would accept nothing more than the tip. Somewhere down the road, a dog barked, and another one, closer, barked back. I moved along the fencerow seeking looser soil, finally finding it near the fence post.

I crouched and dug, prying out thick hunks of pasture grass by the roots to get it out of the way, my hands blistering where they gripped the shovel. It didn't take long to hit something, though the first thing I dug up was a jagged stone. When I pulled it out, I felt something else in the void, something smoother. I carefully worked it loose and brought it into the moonlight. An old-fashioned canning jar, caked with dirt. When I shook it, it made a faint sound like fluttering moths.

I kept going, unearthing more rocks, focused on my work. A low growl came from behind, the sound like the first throat-clearing pull on Daddy's chain saw, the motor gurgling and dying out. I slowly turned around. It was an enormous German shepherd mix that could have passed for a wolf in the dark. One of his ears was shredded, like he'd been in a fight. The dog snarled. I held still, my arms at my sides, and spoke softly. "It's okay. Good boy. Go on home." He started barking, and the more I shushed him, the louder he barked. I tucked the cold, filthy jar in the crook of my arm, held the shovel in front of me, and edged away from the dog, into the field, until I was far enough away to run.

When I got to the car, I found a half-empty bottle of water under the seat and used wet napkins to wipe down the jar. Metal ground against glass as I struggled to unscrew the corroded lid, the blisters on my hands tearing open. Finally I gave up and smashed the jar with a rock, collecting the paper slips inside. Moisture had gotten in, and some of the messages were too stained and degraded to read. I felt guilty sorting through Retta's secrets, looking for Leon's name, and I felt worse the more I read. She described dark feelings that couldn't be prayed away. She confessed to holding hate in her heart for her brother, and for herself. She was filled with a deep well of shame. It was heartbreaking.

Then I came to one that mentioned Pastor Rick. He was the one who had counseled her, helped her heal. On the scrap of paper, she'd written that she wasn't sure at first that what he was doing would help. But she trusted him. When she wouldn't tell him something that Leon had done, he asked her to show him, but she was scared to. *He said only a holy man can make you pure again. One day I'll have to lie with my husband and if I'm not pure, he'll know.* Pastor Rick didn't touch her. He asked her to describe the things that had happened to her, and how they made her feel. Once, he had her close her eyes and lie naked on the floor.

I tried to call Retta on the way home. The first two times it rang and rang, and the third time someone picked up and the line immediately went dead.


I lay in bed thinking about Pastor Rick. I looked over at Sylvie, her eyelids fluttering and her hair spilling over her pillow down to the floor, and I remembered how the pastor had sat on her bed when he came to see me. How he had stroked the yellow blanket and told me that I could talk to him, that he was a very good listener. I fell asleep at some point, and when I woke, sunlight filtered in through the curtains and dappled Sylvie's neatly made bed. There were noises downstairs, cabinets slamming, pans jangling. It was the day before her wedding, and she was already down in the kitchen with Mama, preparing the food for the reception.

I got myself ready and went down to help, dreading what would likely be a full day of cooking and cleaning. They put me to work grinding the meat for ham salad sandwiches, a punishing chore for my blistered hands. I fed chunks of ham into the grinder and turned the crank, watching the meat ooze out of the little holes at the other end like pink worms, and then stirred it together with homemade relish and mayonnaise.

Late in the afternoon, when we had finished making and packing away the sandwiches and potato salad and beans and coleslaw and washed the last of the dishes, I thought I'd be able to slip away, but then Daddy came into the kitchen to announce that we would all sit down together for our final family supper. Tomorrow, Sylvie would become a Blackburn, and I would be going home.

Mama had set aside some extra ham sandwiches for supper, but she didn't complain when Daddy shook his head and said the occasion called for something heartier. After hours of cooking, the last thing I wanted to think about was preparing another meal, but Mama was already pulling out dishes that were barely dry, peeling carrots and chopping greens, heating up the leftover pork belly from the night before. Daddy gave a lengthy blessing and spent most of the meal recounting our family's spiritual journey like it was scripture, with the truck-stop waitress playing Delilah to his Samson, indirectly leading him to a deeper relationship with the Lord.

Mama kept her head bowed. I wondered how many times he

had told this story, if it pained her when he mentioned the waitress, if it took effort not to wince. I'd placed much of the blame
for our upended lives on my mother. She was the daughter of a
tent revival preacher and had always been intensely religious.
Joining Holy Rock was like returning home for her, and she'd
probably been waiting for an excuse to make it happen. But
watching my father lord over the table, mythologizing himself,
it was clear that he had fully embraced his role as the divinely
appointed ruler of our family. I remembered him wrapping his
arms around me after a whipping, telling me that he didn't want
to hurt me, but it was his duty as my father to punish disobedi-
ence, to keep his flock on the righteous path. As though none of
this had been his choice, his fault. I felt sorry now for blaming
only my mother all these years.

When the meal was over, Sylvie and I got up to clear the
table. "Sarabeth!" she said. "Don't worry about the dishes. You'd
better go get your dress."

"Right," I said. "Big day tomorrow."

"Yes it is," Daddy said. "I'm giving away my little girl."

He rose from his seat at the head of the table to embrace my
sister, and then, for the first time since I'd arrived, he held his
arms out to me. I didn't step into them like I'd done automati-
cally all my life, even after a whipping. I didn't move at all. Mama
cleared her throat and Daddy let his arms drop. I had known it
from the time I moved out, but I hadn't truly felt it till now. I'd
had to come back home to believe it. My parents—this place—no
longer held power over me.

On the way to pick up the dress, I took a detour, stopping in
town to get a good-enough signal on my phone so I could look up
the Blackburns' website. It took a bit of searching because I
couldn't recall the exact name, but I finally landed on Rock of

Faith Family Ministries. It was difficult to navigate on the small screen, but I wanted to see what kind of assistance they provided for families and people in need. Specifically, whether they offered counseling for children. It was mentioned in a long list of services and resources. The contact page didn't include the Blackburns' names, phone number, or a physical address, only a form to fill out and submit for more information.

I called Farrow and it went to voicemail. I figured he would be back at work, trying to regroup after everything had fallen apart. I wanted to run something by him before I went to see Minnie, but I didn't have time to wait. The wedding was less than twenty-four hours away, and this was my final night in Wisteria. I told him to check out the ministry, that I was looking at Rick Blackburn rather than Leon. That it might not have anything to do with Abby, but it might have something to do with me. I filled up my tank so I wouldn't run out of gas in the hills at night and headed to the Blackburns' place.

"There you are," Minnie said. "I was beginning to wonder."

I was worried she was going to take me down in the basement again, but she had the dress hanging in the hall closet. It was long and shapeless as a shower curtain. "Looks beautiful," I said.

"You can change in Rachel's room right here," she offered, leading me in. A lamp burned on the nightstand next to the crib, where the baby lay sprawled on her back, asleep, wisps of dark hair framing her face. "All right," Minnie said. "Let's have a look."

I took off my dress and she traded me for the one she'd made. I stepped into it and buttoned it up. It fell all the way to my feet and cinched a bit too tight around the throat. It felt stiff, like she'd starched and ironed it.

"Perfect," she said. "What do you think?"

There was no mirror to see myself, but I didn't need one. "It's . . . lovely," I said. "I can't thank you enough."

She beamed. "Pleased to help. Now, I was just going to have a glass of tea," she said. "Join me."

"I'd love to," I said. "I'll just change out of this so it doesn't get wrinkled." I wasn't sure how I'd wear it all day tomorrow. It felt like it was suffocating me and I'd wanted to rip it off my body within seconds of putting it on.

"Oh, no, it'd be best if you could wear it around a bit, get a sense of whether you need any adjustments."

"Okay." I smiled. "Sure." I followed her to the kitchen and she busied herself getting out glasses and ice. "You know, I've been thinking about those peaches we had the other day, with Sylvie," I said. "They were delicious."

"Thank you," she said. "They're from our own trees."

"I feel impolite asking," I said. "But do you think we could have some with our tea? If you have any left? I've never had any quite that good." I knew we had finished off the jar when I was there before, because I'd watched Sylvie spoon out the last of it when I asked for seconds, and Minnie was too mannerly to deny a guest's request for food.

"I have plenty," she said. "I just need to fetch it from the cellar."

"I can do it," I said. "I don't mind. It's out back, right? I'll let you stay here with the baby."

She looked a little uncertain. "All right. If you don't mind. You'll need the flashlight." She fetched one from the kitchen drawer. "You can go out thataway."

I went out on the back deck and down the steps to the yard. I had to put the flashlight in my armpit and yank open the cellar's wooden door with both hands. I wasn't sure I wanted to go in, but I didn't have time to think about it. I stepped into the dark, cool space and shined the light around. It didn't seem familiar. There were shelves of preserves and not much else. I walked to the far end and squatted down with my back to the wall and closed my eyes. It didn't feel right. And there wasn't any kind of sink or faucet to account for the sound of running water. This wasn't the place where I'd been held.

I was trying to make sense of it, to get the pieces to fit without forcing them together like Farrow and I had done before. The man who held me captive could have raped or killed me if he'd wanted to, but he didn't. That was the part Sheriff Krieger found so hard to believe. But maybe the man had wanted something else.

Not long before I went missing, I had turned down Pastor Rick's offer of counseling. Now I wondered—if he was the man in the mask—if the abduction had been a disturbing attempt to fix me. Maybe he thought fear would make me obedient, that he could transform me through trauma into the sort of girl my parents wanted me to be. And maybe he had satisfied his own perverted urges in the process, looking at my naked body while I was blindfolded, the way he had looked at Retta.

But things got out of hand. He'd grown angry when I fought back, and when the scissors accidentally cut my hair. We all knew the verse from Corinthians. Mama had inscribed it in my prayer book: *But if a woman have long hair, it is a glory to her: for her hair is given her for a covering.* He lost control then, chopping it off, a fitting punishment for a disobedient girl. When I stabbed him, maybe he decided I was beyond saving and just wanted to be rid of me, and that's why he dumped me at the side of the road.

I'd been to the Blackburns' three times now since I'd returned to Wisteria, and I had yet to see Pastor Rick. Farrow had said that Destiny's mother hid her burns under long sleeves. Maybe the pastor was hiding something from me. A scar he didn't want me to see, one that I had carved with the scissors. He wouldn't be able to hide it forever. If I didn't see him tonight, I'd see him at the wedding, standing before the entire congregation, marrying my sister to his son.

I grabbed a jar of peaches, brushed off my dress, and hurried back to the house, where Minnie had the tea waiting. She scooped a generous portion of the fruit into a dessert bowl for me and we sat across from each other at the table. The new dress bunched uncomfortably around the middle when I sat down. I looked around but didn't see my old dress anywhere.

"Finally," she said. "Everything's ready for tomorrow and we can relax and have a proper visit, you and me. Such a busy week."

"Yes," I said. "I can't imagine how you fit everything in— preparing for a wedding, taking care of a baby, helping out with youth group, running a ministry."

I took a bite of peach, sweet and tart, like it had just been plucked fresh from the tree. I hadn't been lying when I flattered her. I could eat the whole jar.

"Well, the ministry's certainly a big undertaking, but it's truly our calling from God. All those years I was waiting for a baby, praying for Him to reveal His plan, and one day it was clear what we had to do. Once I dedicated myself to helping other people's children, along came one of my own. Each of us are instruments of God, *vessels*—we must be willing to serve His purpose, no matter how challenging, no matter what cost." Minnie took a long swallow of tea.

"Ronnie was telling me about the website. He's really proud of his work."

"It's a blessing to have him," she said. "We're not much into technology, but a good ministry has to be able to get the word out and reach the families who need our help. The website was necessary for that. Now we can help troubled children throughout the Ozarks and beyond."

I wondered what she meant by "troubled." Girls like me, who talked back to their parents? Girls who refused arranged marriages? Girls who wanted to get their ears pierced and wear pants? Farrow had said the cases weren't connected after all, but there was something we all had in common. We were "troubled," or troublesome—or at least someone thought so. Abby's adoptive parents called her difficult. Eva Winters had stolen and crashed her parents' car. Destiny's mother had been strict, quick to dole out harsh punishment for the slightest infraction.

Minnie said the ministry reached across the Ozarks and beyond. How many girls would Pastor Rick "help"? I wasn't the first and I wouldn't be the last. Parents frustrated with their children would unknowingly subject them to torture. But it didn't quite make sense. Wouldn't there be too great a risk of someone finding out? Unless . . . the parents already knew. I thought of Trina, Destiny's mother, faking tears while she stoked the fire. She'd known all along where her daughter was. My mother had brought the pastor to talk to me and I'd refused. What if Pastor Rick hadn't snatched me on his own? What if she'd asked him to? Eva's parents said the pastor had sent their daughter on a mission trip, but no one had heard from her. No one was looking for her.

The ministry offered services for families who wanted to fix problem children, or maybe just get rid of them.

I knew Minnie was genuinely passionate about ministering to young girls, trying to mold them in her image and impart the values of chastity and fertility, which she'd clearly succeeded in doing with Sylvie. I believed she could be involved, but surely she wasn't aware of everything her husband was doing. She would never approve of him having sexual contact with underage girls. I had brought Retta's slips of paper to show her, in the pocket of my dress. The dress Minnie had taken from me.

"How did you and the pastor choose Sylvie for Noah?" I said.

She smiled and leaned forward in her seat. "After you left, she was needing someone to look up to. I took her under my wing. Such a good girl. She's strong in her faith." Minnie tilted her head. "It must be hard for you. To see your little sister getting married. But it's not too late for you. You can start a family, too, before you lose out on your best childbearing years."

I forced a polite half smile.

"You haven't touched your tea," she said. Down the hall, the baby squawked and began to cry. "Every time I hear that little cry, I'm reminded what a blessing she is." Minnie craned her neck toward Rachel's room to listen, and just above her collar, I saw a flash of pale, pearly skin. It was puckered like a scar.

I stopped breathing. The baby quieted, and when Minnie turned back to me, whatever I had seen was covered by the collar. I thought of the struggle on the basement floor, when I grabbed the scissors, tried to remember how I'd held them, the angle of the blade as I slashed. Would the mark look like the one on Minnie's neck?

Minnie frowned. I couldn't tell if she'd caught me staring, if the look on my face gave me away. If Minnie was the one I'd stabbed, she and Rick were in it together. He was the one who'd grabbed me at the farm stand. Minnie was the one who'd gotten angry, cut my hair, bashed me in the face hard enough to knock me unconscious. Which one of them had let me go?

"Where's the pastor tonight?" I asked.

The baby's cries grew louder. "Excuse me a moment," she said. "I need to get Rachel."

Minnie disappeared down the back hall and I waited to be sure she was out of sight and then raced as quickly and as quietly as I could to the front door. I felt a rush of relief as I hit the porch and eased the door shut behind me, but when I reached the bottom of the steps and started to run for my car, I realized that I was too late. My car wasn't where I'd left it. It was gone, and my phone along with it.

# CHAPTER 28

# SARABETH, THEN

## AGE 18

My father brought me home from the station in the middle of the night and Mama hurried me up to bed, whispering so as not to wake anyone. Sylvie wasn't there, and Mama said she'd taken to sleeping in her and Daddy's room. I fell asleep almost immediately from sheer exhaustion but woke at dawn, too anxious to stay in bed. Mama heard me on the stairs and whisked me back into my room, insisting that I needed to rest. She brought fresh biscuits and a glass of milk and made sure the curtains were shut tight.

There was nothing to fill the time. I stared at the shelf where my books had once been. All that remained was the *Guide for Godly Girls*. I opened it up, but most of the pages were missing. Mama had removed the ones I'd defaced, probably worried that the number of the Beast would open a door for the Devil. Sylvie had half a dozen of the homemade journals stacked neatly on the dresser on her side of the room. When the shelf paper ran out, Mama had started covering them with remnants of Christmas wrapping. I had never peeked to see how Sylvie filled all those pages, because I liked to pretend we had some measure of privacy in our room, though there was no doubt Mama would have read them. I picked up the one at the top of the stack, recognizing the red-and-green paper from the package of shelled walnuts the Darlings had gifted us last Christmas.

The journal was filled with Sylvie's careful handwriting, and as I flipped through the pages, I spotted my name. Fissures formed in my heart as I read her prayers. *Dear Lord, please help my sister Sarabeth to be good.*

I could hear people from church as they came by with offerings. They brought deer steaks and freshly plucked chickens and cured ham. And guns: shotguns and rifles and revolvers, enough for every member of the family to carry one in each hand. That was what people did in difficult times, provide prayer and sustenance and firepower. My father accepted the meat with gratitude and politely declined the weapons, explaining that he and Eli had hunting rifles and that should be enough to protect the house.

His voice was strong and unwavering. He didn't sound worried that we were in any danger. *You were let go,* he'd said matter-of-factly on the ride home, as though that meant the ordeal was over. It felt like he was disappointed in me somehow. Neither of my parents came right out and said they didn't believe me, like Sheriff Krieger had, but they seemed to have their doubts.

When night came, I slept fitfully. I wished Sylvie could have been there in the room with me, but Mama had insisted that I needed peace and quiet to recover, even though the last thing I wanted after a week of silent solitude was to be alone. She acted as though my well-being was her foremost concern, but it felt like an excuse to keep me isolated from my brothers and sister, as though she feared my mere presence would somehow taint them.

The next day, the reporters came. They descended on the farm with their vans and cameras and antennas. They knocked on the door. The phone rang and rang and rang until someone unplugged it. I heard my mother praying for them to go away and leave us in peace. There was another knock at the door, one that my parents answered. I peeked out through the curtains and saw a police cruiser. Later, when Mama brought up a lukewarm bowl of bean soup for dinner, she told me that I would have to go back to the police station in the morning, that one of the deputies would come to fetch me.

I didn't want to go to the police station and have Sheriff Krieger ask me the same questions all over again, each one punctuated by an irritable sigh. I couldn't stay in my room forever, nor could I imagine what would happen when they let me out. Maybe my parents would move forward with the arranged marriage as though nothing had changed, or maybe no one would want to marry me now, whether they believed my story or not. Maybe I would be a pariah in my own home. Retta hadn't called or come to check on me, and neither had Tom, though both Retta's mother and Mrs. Darling had stopped by to bring us food. I didn't know whether my friends hadn't wanted to come along or hadn't been allowed.

I lay in bed thinking about how, years before, in our old house in town, my family had watched reruns of *The Waltons* together on television. On the show, at bedtime, the Walton children would call out good night to one another until their father told them to be quiet and go to bed. Eli and I had started to do the same thing, as a joke. *Good night, Eli! Good night, Sarabeth!*

*Good night, Mama! Good night, Daddy!* We hadn't done that in a very long time. Sylvie didn't even remember *The Waltons,* nor did my little brothers.

"Good night, Eli," I said to the darkness. "Good night, Mama. Good night, Daddy." No one answered.

## CHAPTER 29

# SARAH, NOW

Panic tingled through my limbs and I tried to shake it off. Minnie wouldn't have had time to move my car while I was in the root cellar, so the pastor was around here somewhere. I couldn't stay out in the open, so I ran for the cover of the trees and hid among the pines. It was miles to the main road from here, maybe twenty more to town, but there must be houses down the other dirt roads, someplace I could find a phone, if I could navigate the woods in the dark. If they didn't find me first.

Or there was Ronnie. I didn't know if I could trust him—if he was in on their plans, whatever they were—but he would have a truck, and a phone, and maybe I could get to one or the other. His trailer was only a half mile away.

I crept between the trees, feeling my way, barely any moonlight making its way to the uneven ground. I wasn't used to the cumbersome skirt swishing against my legs, catching on thorns and vines. I stopped to listen and didn't hear anyone following me, but as I got closer to Ronnie's, I could hear the dogs over the ventilation fans. They were barking and howling and rattling the cages. It occurred to me that the kennel would be a perfect place to hide someone—the animal noise would mask any other sounds. I moved closer to the road so I could get a look and saw a shadow moving around the side of the building. Parked in front of Ronnie's trailer were two vehicles: his truck and my car. It had been a stupid risk. I'd wasted time and now I had to go back the way I'd come.

I needed to avoid the road, where I might be spotted, and I knew I'd get disoriented quickly if I slipped deeper into the woods, but all that mattered to me now was that I get away. There was little chance they'd find me in the acres of wilderness, and I could hide until daylight and hike my way out.

I spun around at the sound of my name. Someone was calling for me. Not *Sarah*, but *Sarabeth*, drawing out the syllables, hollering from a ways off, and I walked in what I hoped was the opposite direction. I wondered if Sylvie would be worried when I didn't come home, or if Minnie or my parents would tell her I'd left again without saying goodbye, that I couldn't stand to watch her marry Noah.

I tried to move as quietly as I could, biting my tongue when branches caught my hair and clawed my face. A car engine squealed and I couldn't tell where it was coming from, how close it was. I had angled away from Ronnie's, heading north, but apparently I hadn't angled enough or hadn't kept a steady course, because the back of the old farmhouse appeared through a break in the trees.

I turned away from it and heard a sharp crack, a stick snapping. I held my breath, my eyes wide, waiting, watching. There was a soft rustling and I saw something move. I ran toward the old house, not knowing where else to go. It was dark inside, no lights burning, so I tried the back door and it squeaked open far enough to slip in.

I peeked out the window and didn't see anyone coming after me. Maybe it had been an animal moving in the woods, a deer. I pushed a chair against the door and looked for a landline phone but didn't see one. There were a few pieces of furniture and little else. This was the Blackburns' old house, the guesthouse that Ronnie said was used for the ministry. It didn't look like anyone was staying at the house now, but I couldn't hide out here. If there wasn't anyone waiting for me when I checked the rear window, I'd run back into the woods and keep going.

I glanced around the room one last time to see if anything might be useful as a weapon, and a door caught my attention. I'd seen it when I first came in but hadn't looked closely in the dark. Now everything else fell away and it didn't matter that Minnie and Ronnie and the pastor might be circling the house that very moment, blocking my escape. I didn't know if the door led to a closet or bathroom or a furnace or a set of stairs, but it was locked from the outside with a sliding bar and a deadbolt, and I knew that I couldn't leave without opening it and seeing what lay behind it.

I slid the bar, twisted the lock, and swung the door open. A set of stairs led down into absolute darkness. I felt around for a switch and found it but couldn't risk anyone seeing the light from outside. I stepped into the stairwell and shut the door firmly behind me, sealing myself inside, unable to breathe until I flicked on the light. I descended the plank steps, holding tight to the rail, and the first thing I saw at the bottom was a utility sink with a laundry bar hanging above it. My head swam. I had never seen this room before, but I remembered it.

I bit down hard on my tongue to quell the rush of panic so I could focus. To the right I spotted two doors, both locked from the outside like the one upstairs. I staggered to the first one and knocked. "Is anyone in there?" Something slammed into the door from the other side.

"Let me the fuck out!"

I unlocked the door and a girl with long black hair and freckles stared back at me. She eyed my dress suspiciously. It was identical to the one she wore. "Who are you?"

"Sarah. Are you . . . Eva?"

"How do you know me?"

"I—"

"I don't care." She shook her shackled wrist in my face. "If you're here to help, hurry up. The key's on a hook by the sink." I ran to get it while she pounded on the wall between the two rooms. "Abby! Come on, we're getting out."

*Abby.* The name sent a shiver through my bones. I gave Eva the key and hurried to open the other door. The girl inside backed into the corner, eyes wide. I recognized her face from the picture Farrow had given me the day we met. "Abby Donnelly," I said. "We've been looking for you." Eva pushed past me to remove Abby's shackle and then we rushed up the stairs, Eva dragging Abby behind her.

"Hold on to me," I said. "I have to turn off the light before we open the door."

"Where're we going?" Eva hissed.

"Out the back of the house to the woods. If it's clear, we run."

I switched off the light and turned the knob. The door creaked open and I blinked, my eyes still adjusting, straining to map shapes in the darkness.

"Shit," Eva whispered in my ear. "He with you?"

It was Noah. He blocked the back door, a rifle cradled in his arms.

"Come on," he said. "They're looking for you."

I didn't move. Abby and Eva huddled behind me on the stairs, holding tight to my dress, and I could feel them breathing, the thud of their heartbeats moving through me.

"I'll help you."

"You trust him?" Eva murmured.

"I don't know."

"I got you out before," Noah said.

"What?"

"Last time. It was me."

My skin prickled. "How do I know you're not lying?"

He moved closer. "I came back early from a prayer retreat my dad sent me on, and the basement door was open, blood on the steps. They were upstairs, yelling, didn't hear me come in. I found you hog-tied and got you to the truck. When I pulled you out, I lost my grip and you got cut on the door. Here." He pressed his palm to his hip and I could feel it on my own body, the outline of my scar. "I laid you down and made sure you were breathing before I left."

Noah. He was the one who'd set me free. He was the one who'd leaned over me, listening for my breath, not to make sure I was dead, but that I was still alive.

I stepped over the threshold, the girls squeezing through the doorway with me. "Let's go."

"Stay close," Noah said.

We followed him outside, to the corner of the house. As he peered around the edge, a shot rang out. He flattened himself against the wall and motioned for us to get down. Someone ran toward us from the other side of the house and Noah popped up and aimed the rifle.

The woman saw us girls first in our pale gowns and then froze when she spotted Noah. I could tell she wasn't with the Blackburns. She was dressed in a dark hoodie and cargo pants, a bandana over her hair. She held her hands up in front of her, and I noticed they were perfectly steady, no tremors, despite the gun in her face. She was close enough that I could make out a mark on her wrist. A tattoo. It was a paw print, same as Melissa's, and I knew who she was. She'd gotten my tip about the dogs, had come to scout it out, just like Melissa said.

"She can help us," I said. "You're with the animal rescue, right? Melissa gave me your number. I sent you the map." The hard line of her mouth softened when she heard Melissa's name, and she blew out a pent-up breath and nodded. "Where's your car? We need to get out of here."

The woman glanced at us in turn, Abby sobbing quietly, Eva looking ready to tear someone's throat out, Noah gripping the rifle. "Just them," Noah said. "Can you drive them out?"

"Yeah," she said. Whatever she thought was going on, she seemed okay with escaping first and asking questions later. She fished a walkie-talkie out of her pocket and held it up. "My partner's in a van outside the gate."

"I'll get the gate open and keep them from coming after you," Noah said. "Stick to the woods till you're sure it's safe."

He eased around the corner and waved for us to go, and we ran. Moments later, there was another gunshot, and another. Each one made my heart jump, but I didn't look back. We had just made it into the trees when Eva buckled and sank to the ground.

"You hurt?" I bent to pull her up and saw a dark smear on her dress. It looked like blood. "We're almost there," I whispered. "Come on."

"She okay?" the woman asked. "Wayne can help, he's a vet." She clicked the walkie-talkie. "Gate should be opening, I need you here now. I've got three kids with me. One of 'em's injured."

We followed the edge of the woods until we neared the driveway, then started running when we heard the van. Abby and I dragged Eva between us. The van barreled toward us and skidded to a stop in the gravel. The woman flung open the sliding door.

"Gina! I heard shots."

"Get in back!" she hollered at Wayne. "I'm driving." He gaped at us as we piled in. Gina shoved him. "Help her! I'll call 911." Wayne scrambled into the back while Gina swung the van around and sped down the road.

Eva was doubled over, clinging to Abby's hand. "Here, can you lie down?" Wayne said. He aimed the light from his phone. Eva's dress was stained with blood. "Where does it hurt?"

"My stomach."

"Somebody hold the light." I grabbed the phone. He felt along her abdomen, frantically seeking a wound, fighting to pull up the voluminous skirt and get it out of the way. He stopped suddenly, sucked in his lip. "Is there any chance you're pregnant?"

"Maybe," Eva said, her jaw clenched.

"You might be having a miscarriage. We'll have to get you to a doctor."

"Was it the pastor?" I asked.

Eva looked at me and spit her words through gritted teeth. "That's Ronnie's job. Pastor'd do it himself if he could get it up. He promised Minnie more babies."

"But she has Rachel, and she just told me she thought she had another on the way."

"Another on the way?" Eva grimaced and glanced down, her bloodstained hands pressed to her stomach. "She was talking about me. *My* babies. Rachel's mine."

"Oh god . . . so your parents thought the Blackburns were sending you on a mission trip, but really they were just . . . keeping you here? For this?"

"No." She struggled into a sitting position, leaning on Abby. "My parents knew the mission trip was fake. That whole thing was a cover. They brought me here when they found out I was pregnant. They just wanted to get rid of me. The Blackburns were nice at first, said they'd help me. They were all about tough love, but Minnie was sweet to me. Talked to me about giving the baby up for adoption—she always wanted more kids of her own. But Rick started up with some creepy shit, coming in my room at night to check on me. Walked in one time when I was in the bathtub and put his hand on my belly . . . said he needed to 'examine' me, see how far along I was. I knew it'd only get worse from there. Later, I told Minnie what happened, told her I had to leave, and she poured me a glass of sweet tea so we could talk it over. Woke up the next day in the basement. When Rachel was born, Minnie took her for herself. Then she figured, if she could have one, why not more? She said it was God's will—that this was my purpose. I was a *vessel.*"

So that was Minnie's big revelation after years of faith and prayer and steadfast struggle, the answer she'd been looking for. I remembered her talking about each of us having a purpose, being vessels. She'd found out what her husband was doing with the girls he was "counseling"—it had been going on for years, since Retta, at least, and maybe before. When Eva threatened to leave, Minnie might have worried she would tell. She couldn't risk losing everything—her husband, the church, the ministry, and definitely not the baby that was finally within her reach. She must have convinced herself that this was God's plan, His wisdom at last revealed: that the girls her husband brought into their home could serve a greater purpose. If they could feed his fetish, they could give her what she wanted, too. She'd suffered long enough as the barren wife of the pastor and decided it was time to claim her due.

"How'd you get here, Abby?"

"My mother kept locks on everything." Her voice was soft and halting. "The refrigerator. My bedroom door. I snuck out my window one night and she caught me stealing food from our neighbor's trash. Said she couldn't handle me anymore and she brought me here."

"So who are you?" Eva asked me. "You said you were looking for Abby. How did you know where to find us?"

"I was in that basement, too, before you."

I almost said "same as you," but that wasn't quite true. I hadn't been subjected to the same horrors they had. Maybe the Blackburns were still figuring things out when they took me, thinking they were truly helping families—that they could somehow transform me into the obedient daughter my parents wanted me to be. It had felt like they were getting me ready for something the night I escaped—maybe they were preparing to take me home before I fought back and Noah found me. But if they had returned me to my doorstep as they'd likely planned, the police wouldn't have been called. My parents would have kept it quiet, a family secret. I wouldn't have ended up on the news. I wouldn't have gotten the help I needed to work through the trauma and start over again on my own. I might never have left Wisteria.

The difference between me and Abby and Eva was that my parents were expecting me back. Pastor Rick had been abusing children for a long time, but at some point, as their ministry grew, the Blackburns must have recognized that there were no limits when it came to girls who would not be missed, girls with no place else to go.

Eva had said she blacked out after drinking Minnie's tea, the same tea, perhaps, that Minnie had offered me tonight. What would have happened if I'd taken a sip? Would I have ended up back in the basement? She could have told my family I'd returned to the city, and they would have believed it. But back home, in St. Agnes, my absence would raise alarms. I had people waiting for me. Helen and Melissa would report me missing. Farrow would come looking, and he wouldn't give up until he found me.

"Ambulance'll take an hour," Gina hollered from the front. "I can get us there quicker."

Wayne, who'd been sitting in stunned silence, roused at the sound of Gina's voice. "You girls need to call somebody?" he said.

Neither Eva nor Abby replied. "I do," I said. I still had Wayne's phone in my hand. I didn't know Farrow's number by heart, so I did a quick search and dialed the Missouri State Highway Patrol.

# CHAPTER 30

# SARABETH, THEN

## AGE 18

Deputy Willis came to pick me up and my parents watched me go, my mother handing me my Bible as I walked out the door. I was grateful, at least, that I didn't have to ride in a car with Sheriff Krieger. His mocking voice twanged in my head, sharp as a pinched nerve. Deputy Willis was quiet. He said nothing on the way into town, his lips moving to an old Hank Williams song on the radio. When we arrived at the station, he escorted me inside. Two women were waiting. One was a county social worker, a stout gray-haired woman in a polyester pant-suit. The other, a younger woman with thick red curls, intro-duced herself as a victim advocate from the Midwest Victims Advocacy Network. They guided me into a room and closed the door, leaving Deputy Willis out in the hall. The three of us sat down.

"I'm sorry you were alone before," the advocate said. Her name was Leah, and she wore a denim dress and ankle boots. "We should have been notified."

Tears flooded down my face. It was the first time I'd cried

since opening my eyes at the rest stop. I realized that I hadn't teared up once during the hours of interrogation or exams, or when I was reunited with my family.

The social worker opened her bag and handed me a packet of tissues. She took out a clipboard and pen. As Leah discussed the various services and resources available to me as the victim of a violent crime, she spoke of decisions, plans. It took me a while to realize that she wasn't telling me what was going to happen. She was asking me what I wanted to do.

"Now, I have a few standard questions that I need to ask," she said. "This is confidential. Do you feel safe at home?"

My mouth opened but no words came out. I was used to smiling and cheerily replying that I was doing well, if anyone asked, but this question caught me off guard. I'd expected her to ask about the abuse I'd endured in captivity, or the interrogation afterward. No one ever questioned what went on behind closed doors in our home. Family matters were private, and living as we did, there was no one to intervene.

"It's okay," she said. "Just answer truthfully." Her warm words were like a hand reaching out. All I had to do was grasp it.

"No," I said. "I don't feel safe at home. Or in this police station, or this town. I need to get out of here, but I don't think my parents will let me leave."

My words filled the room, floating in the air, swelling up like balloons ready to burst.

"You're eighteen years old now," the social worker said, squinting at her paperwork. "You don't need permission."

My birthday had come and gone without mention, forgotten in the chaos, but it hadn't escaped the notice of this woman with her forms. I'd looked forward to turning eighteen for so long, thinking I'd finally be free, only to discover my parents had something else in store for me. But outside of their house, beyond their control, the number still had meaning.

Leah crossed her legs, the hem of her dress riding up above her knees. Her bare skin was dotted with bright freckles. "If you need a safe place to go," she said, "we can help you."

In the windowless room, I began to see a way out. It was a dark tunnel, and I didn't know what lay on the other side, but all that mattered was that I'd end up someplace better. I thought of my bedroom, the bare shelf, the blank walls. I looked at these two women, both strangers, armed with nothing but paperwork and tissues. Angels, of a sort. The kind you could count on. I opened my Bible and removed the picture of Sylvie that I'd tucked between the pages. I wondered, when my mother handed the book to me, if she knew I wouldn't be back.

## CHAPTER 31

# SARAH, NOW

Each room in the house glowed with color. My kitchen was the green of spring fields, my living room the blue of an old canning jar, my bedroom a soft shade of peach called Sunrise. When I had mentioned to Helen that I was finally going to paint over all the splotches, she'd told Melissa, who told everyone at work, and from there it turned into a painting party, with pizza and beer and music playing. Karim had come, and the other vet techs, and the girls from the front desk. The house looked different when we were done, and it felt different, too. Melissa couldn't believe I didn't have any pictures to hang on the walls, so she made us take a group selfie that she printed and framed for me. I'd hung it in the kitchen next to the chalkboard, which was no longer pristine: I had written down an appointment to do something very important with Helen. It fell exactly one month after the day that would have been Sylvie's wedding.

Helen had offered to keep Gypsy when I returned from Wisteria, not wanting me to be overwhelmed after everything that had happened, but I missed her. She still hadn't received any applications for adoption. When I asked Melissa if she'd allow me a foster fail, she said it was about time. She brought a doggy cake to the office to celebrate Gypsy's adoption and sent us home with a new foster: Mr. Marmalade, the skinny orange cat who hated being locked up in a cage. He was gradually calming down with an entire house to roam through, though he still ran for the door every time I opened it. I couldn't blame him.

Farrow and I talked or messaged nearly every day. He was busy with Abby, making sure she got the help she needed, working on a plan for what would come next. They were getting to know each other again, as family. He was in touch with Eva, too, who was in a temporary foster home along with Rachel. He hoped that I would be able to connect with both of them soon, that it might be helpful for the three of us to talk to one another about what we had been through. Three invisible girls whose families had never reported them missing, whose disappearances went largely unnoticed until they were found.

Abby and Eva's treatment in the news was kinder than mine had been five years before. They had passed the test for Girls Who Come Back, their unbelievable stories proven beyond doubt by witnesses and evidence. Ronnie confessed to assaulting Eva, though he claimed he'd only done it at the direction of Pastor Rick, who told him it was a mission from God. He hadn't touched Abby; the pastor was saving her for himself. I had evidence, too, finally, and belated vindication: five years after Sheriff Krieger had accused me of lying, the blood on my slip was matched to Minnie Blackburn.

I mourned the other invisible girls, the ones who remained missing, their bones hidden in firepits and basements and forests and farm ponds, betrayed by those who should have protected them. I wished that Destiny had not been among them. In her

interrogation, Trina's self-righteous rambling had yielded a motive, if not a confession. *That day comes when a man's eye slides
past you and lands on your daughter. I had to protect her from all
of that. It's a mother's job.* I didn't buy that she had killed Destiny
to protect her. If she truly thought her boyfriend was preying on
her daughter—and there was no indication that he was—it
would have made more sense to kill Vance. Whether Trina was
jealous of Destiny for reasons real or imagined, she had chosen
her boyfriend over her flesh and blood, and set her own child on
fire. I could still picture her singing hymns in the prayer circle,
stoking the fire as it burned.


Farrow and I finally got a chance to catch up in person, just the
two of us, a few weeks after he'd raced to meet Gina's van at the
hospital in Branson. We greeted each other with a brief hug
when he walked into the coffee shop, and I remembered how
he'd swept me into his arms in the hallway at the hospital, how
we'd clung to each other beneath the fluorescent lights. I'd
thought about that moment a lot in the days since, the warmth of
him, the way he looked at me. He had whispered that I was safe,
and for once I believed it, felt it in my bones.

As we sipped our coffee and he filled me in on the progress of
the case, he paused and looked at me with the same endearing
half smile he'd flashed the first time I met him. "We make a good
team," he said. There was a palpable energy between us, and my
breath grew shallow in anticipation. "Have you ever considered
a career in law enforcement?"

I stared at him for a moment, then burst out laughing.

"I'm not joking," he said. "You've got the instincts for it. You'd
be a natural."

"It's not that," I said. "I thought you were going to say something else."

"What?"

"Nothing. It's embarrassing."

He raised an eyebrow, waiting. "I hope you know by now that you can tell me anything."

"Fine," I said. "I thought you were going to ask me out."

He set down his cup. "Would you have laughed if I did?"

"No."

"Would you have said yes?"

"I guess we'll never know."

He laughed into his hand. "Okay. We can be completely honest with each other, right? I look forward to talking to you every day. I save all your texts, like some kind of psychopath, in case I want to go back and reread them. I couldn't wait to get here this morning to see you. And I would love to take you out. It's just that . . . I don't know if that's a line we should cross. Considering how we met, and everything you've been through . . . I don't want to do anything to make you uncomfortable, to pressure you. You deserve to have normal relationships that don't revolve around criminal investigations. And you deserve to go on a real first date with someone you care about. Maybe to a restaurant where rolls aren't being thrown at your head."

"I didn't mind the rolls," I said. "They were good."

"Yeah. They were."

"I appreciate your concern," I said. "And I think we should go for it. You said I could have a do-over, remember? I kind of feel like you owe me."

The corner of his mouth turned up. "You sure about this?"

"It's just a date," I said. "It's not like we're getting married. If it doesn't feel right, we'll go back to whatever we are now."

"All right. Where do you want to go?"

"You can't laugh," I said.

"I won't."

"You laugh sometimes when it's inappropriate."

"I promise," he said.

"I've always wanted to go to Olive Garden," I said.

"Why did you think I'd laugh? Endless breadsticks are no joke."

"*And* . . . maybe roller skating after, if you're up for it."

"Sounds perfect," he said.


Things remained unsettled with my family. My parents were sorry but not in the ways I wanted them to be. They still insisted that they'd done what they thought was best, fearing my soul was in jeopardy, and their own souls if they couldn't save me. They had trusted the Blackburns to help me and had no idea what torturous methods they would use. Pastor Rick had called them the night I got away and fed them a story. That I'd fought every effort they put forth, that I'd harmed myself and threatened them and had to be restrained. That Noah had stumbled in and misunderstood the situation, and I'd suffered further injuries in my escape before ending up at the side of a road in such dramatic fashion. My parents worried that I was a lost cause, a danger to my own family. And that was why they let me go, believing they'd tried everything and failed. I wasn't sure I could forgive them, but I buried their apology like a seed in my heart, to give it time.

I hadn't spoken to Sylvie, though I'd tried. Mama would only say that she was distraught, and I didn't know how much of that was due to the cancellation of her wedding, and whether she blamed me, somehow, for ruining her plans. Sylvie had been so close to Minnie, so excited to become a Blackburn. Part of me wondered just how much she knew about their ministry, how deeply she'd been involved. I pushed down a darker thought, that maybe she knew everything, including what they'd done to me.

Noah had helped me escape not once, but twice, and I would always be grateful, though I couldn't help thinking how different things would have been if he'd turned his parents in the first time. In generous moments, I could understand why he hadn't. He'd taken a risk as it was, getting me out of that house and setting me free, defying his parents. He'd been grazed by a bullet and returned fire on his own family to protect me and two girls he didn't know. I understood now why he'd seemed angry when he saw me in the kitchen with Minnie. He knew what she'd done to me before and wouldn't let it happen again. He hadn't known about the other girls; Rick and Minnie had waited until he moved out to bring another one home. Noah had always seemed an uneasy fit in his family, uninterested in playing the role of the pastor's son. His parents had been trying to draw him back into the fold, building him a home, pushing him to marry Sylvie, but now that they were in custody, maybe he could finally be free of their influence and expectation and live life on his own terms. He deserved that as much as anyone.

I worried that things would be awkward at work now that everyone knew who I was and what had happened, but my first day back I realized it was actually easier to talk to people when I wasn't trying to hide a secret. It helped that Melissa monopolized the conversation, focusing on the dogs that had been rescued from the Blackburns' puppy mill and taking some of the spotlight off me. For the first time, I ate lunch in the break room instead of my office, something my counselor, Casey, had been recommending since I'd started working there. Karim invited me to sit with him and the other techs, and I only froze up for a moment before saying yes.

It was clear and sunny the morning Helen came to the shelter to pick me up for our appointment. Her car was every bit as glamorous as it appeared in foster photos, only instead of a carsick Chihuahua in the front seat, I was there, only slightly nauseated. I sank into the ivory leather, inhaling Helen's vetiver perfume.

"You sure you're ready for this?" she said.

"I hope so."

Everything in the store was candy colored, pink and lavender and aqua. There were sparkly lip glosses, furry phone cases, unicorn headbands. Melissa had argued that I should go to a tattoo parlor downtown that had professional body piercers, but Helen said it was more than okay to indulge my childhood dream of going to a mall and sitting on a glittery throne to get my ears pierced.

As I watched the two little girls going before me, I heard my mother's scornful voice, preaching about what kind of girl would do such a thing. I tuned it out. The girls giggled, grinning at each other. The young woman doing the piercing smiled brightly and told them they were brave. She held the gun with a steady hand. When my turn came, she gave me a stuffed bear to squeeze.

"You got this," Helen said, taking out her phone. "We'll get ice cream after."

"Don't tell me you're taking pictures."

"Come on, you know me better than that. This is a big deal! You can't *not* take pictures. This is going on the foster page."

I groaned and Helen laughed. At the last second, I squeezed my eyes shut, braced for the pinch, but it was over before I knew it.

"So?" Helen said. "How do you feel?"

"Different," I said. My ears stung. I held up the mirror to see. The silver studs were barely noticeable, but I felt changed. Like I'd reclaimed a bit of my old self, the Sarabeth before the farm, and glimpsed a new me that I didn't fully recognize—not quite the person I had been or the one I wanted to be, but still in progress, somewhere in between.

I returned to work afterward, where Melissa examined my earlobes and declared that the holes had been sufficiently centered. I was typing an email when the phone rang, the number unknown. I breathed in the scent of wet dogs and disinfectant, pressed my palm to the desk, focused on the enormous Lambert's mug that Farrow had given me. It said HEADS UP! in bold caps, and it made me smile to think of the flying rolls. The mug was filled to the brim with cold water, but I didn't need it. My mouth hadn't gone dry. I blew out my breath and reached for the phone, unafraid of what might await me at the other end of the line. There were no more secrets to be dredged up out of the dark, no more skeletons resting uneasily in shallow graves— only the same things everyone fears, the ordinary monsters that might come for anyone in the light of day.

# ACKNOWLEDGMENTS

Thank you, as always, to my family—Harper, Piper, Brent, and all my supportive relatives and in-laws—and my dear friends. I love you all. I'm grateful to Lisa, Diane, Ellen, and Mom for being early readers and encouraging me. Special thanks to Elizabeth, Hilary, Angie, Amy, Emily, Sally, Liz, and Adonica, and many thanks to Mark and Emma Beary, who humor me when I text pictures of bones to ask if they are human. (So far, no, but I always feel like I should check.) Thank you, Mark, for generously sharing your knowledge of forensics.

I'm lucky to have great writing friends, and it all started with Jill Orr, Jen Gravley, Nina Furstenau, Ann Breidenbach, and Allison Smythe. Thank you to Amy Engel, Karen Katchur, Julia Dahl, and Jocelyn Cullity for always being willing to talk writing with me.

Thank you to everyone at Random House who worked on this book, especially my editor, Andrea Walker, Emma Caruso, Allyson Lord, Colleen Nuccio, and Amy Ryan, and big thanks to my agent, Sally Wofford-Girand.

Thank you to Lena Acton for surprising me at the library in St. Louis and telling me one last time that you were proud of me.

Special shout-out to reader Becky Sandusky, who had my first book, *The Weight of Blood*, tattooed on her arm. As a writer, nothing means more than knowing your work has resonated with someone.

Finally, huge and heartfelt thanks to all the librarians, book-sellers, bloggers, and readers out there. None of this happens without you and your love of books.

## ABOUT THE AUTHOR

Laura McHugh is the internationally bestselling author of *The Weight of Blood*, winner of an International Thriller Writers Award and a Killer Nashville Silver Falchion Award for best first novel; *Arrowood*, an International Thriller Writers Award finalist for best novel; and *The Wolf Wants In*. McHugh lives in Missouri with her husband and daughters.

Facebook.com/lauramchughauthor
Twitter: @LauraSMcHugh
Instagram: @lauramchughauthor

## ABOUT THE TYPE

This book was set in Electra, a typeface designed for Linotype by W. A. Dwiggins, the renowned type designer (1880–1956). Electra is a fluid typeface, avoiding the contrasts of thick and thin strokes that are prevalent in most modern typefaces.